BREATH PLAY

A Dan Burnett Thriller

BY

LARRY TERHAAR

Praise for *AGAINST THE BLUE WALL...*

"*Against the Blue Wall* is a must-read for anyone who wants to understand the realities of police violence and the difficulty of seeking justice within a flawed system. It's perfect for fans of social justice thrillers, true crime enthusiasts, and readers who aren't afraid to confront uncomfortable truths. If you're looking for a book that will challenge you, anger you, and make you think, this one is it."

— *Literary Titan Review*

"5 out of 5 stars. The story takes off like a rocket, with nonstop action and suspense. The characters are very well-defined, and the storyline, sadly, is only too real in today's society. Great read. Next??"

— J.C., *NetGalley*

"Libraries will find *Against the Blue Wall's* action, characters, and perceptions lend to a thoroughly engrossing thriller. Readers and book clubs intrigued by PI investigations that explore police action and prejudice will find this book a riveting winner."

— D. Donovan, Sr. Reviewer, *Midwest Book Review*

"Dan Burnett is on the case again! Filled with memorable Characters and a hefty dose of suspense, Larry Terhaar's newest thriller will keep you turning the page."

—Prill Boyle, author of *Defying Gravity*

Hat City
Publishing

CHAPTER 1

I called 911 from my cell phone, told them where I was, and what I had found. After being connected to the Mamaroneck Police Department, I repeated it all to the desk Sergeant, who took my name and number. Having no desire to remain near the smell any longer, I made my way back along the beach and found Mia sitting on a log, patiently waiting for my return.

"What is it, Dan?" Mia asked.

"It's a human body wrapped in a blanket. Judging from the smell, I'd guess it's been in the water for quite some time."

"Oh my God!" She pulled the collar of her shirt over her nose. Her eyes locked on mine as if begging me to tell her it wasn't true. "A dead body on Mamaroneck Beach?"

"Yeah. Let's head back to the house—the police have my number if they want to speak with me again."

Mia and I had been walking westward on the beach, upwind with the sun on our faces, just a block downhill from her house in Mamaroneck, New York.

We had watched the seagulls flying over the surf, calling to one another as they hunted for anything edible. Their wings glinted in the sunlight as they dove and glided across the surface. If they found something inside a shell, they would snatch it, work their wings skyward, and then drop it on the rocky shore, in hopes of bursting the shell open to reveal their prize.

Early September in the Northeast can bring a wide variety of weather. This day was perfect, with a temperature of seventy-eight degrees, sunny, and a light breeze. Dressed in shorts, T-shirts, and sneakers, we had walked about a mile when I got the first hint of the odor and saw the seagulls swarming around something at the water's edge. Mia had yet to notice it.

A few moments later, I caught the scent again and immediately knew the source—I was all too familiar with the odor of decaying flesh. When Mia noticed the foul odor, I suggested she stay put while I investigated. She found a large driftwood log nearby to sit on while I headed for what had attracted the birds.

I spotted a lump rolling back and forth in the surf, and when I was within fifty yards, I saw something rolled up in a gray blanket tied on each end with heavy rope. Judging from its size, I knew it was a human body, and went no further. That was when I called 911.

Now, with the wind behind us, I led Mia down the beach with my arm around her while she came to grips with what we had just found. I knew the beach was Mia's sanctuary, and her silence told me how much her world had just been rocked. It was a leisurely stroll back to her house, except for the last hundred yards, pumping our legs up the hill.

Once inside, we sat in the living room at the rear of her house, overlooking the beach and Long Island Sound. We called it our happy place, on the couch in front of a wall of glass doors, where we had shared our first kiss nearly a year ago. It was about time for cocktail hour, a daily ritual we enjoyed in this spot. I shook up a batch of Manhattans in the kitchen, poured them into martini glasses with a burgundy cherry and a twist of orange peel, then returned to our happy place, hoping the drink would calm her.

My name is Dan Burnett. I was a detective with the NYPD for thirty years before retiring last fall due to a bad back. Besides that, I'm in pretty good shape for fifty-five and still have a full head of brown hair. At 6'3" and 180 pounds on a lanky frame, I've been told I appear to be all elbows and knees. Since retiring, I'd become a private detective, which is how I met Mia—she hired me to investigate her brother's murder.

Mia is seven years younger than I, and a widow of four years. She and her late husband owned this classic home on the north shore of Long Island Sound that became hers when he died after a two-year battle with cancer. I was attracted to Mia the moment I met her. Her beauty was effortless, yet she made a conscious effort not to draw attention to herself by wearing minimal makeup and comfortable clothing. Her dark brown hair cascaded naturally over her shoulders, and her eyes had gold sparkles in a sea of green. It was a struggle not to become romantically involved with her while she was my client. After solving her brother's murder, we began a passionate affair.

Since we became a couple, I've been fortunate to live in this beautiful home with her, especially over the winter. My home was a forty-three-foot sailboat docked on City Island. After my divorce a few years ago, I began sleeping there and came to enjoy it; there was a certain sense of adventure to living on a boat.

When she'd taken the first sip of her Manhattan, Mia said, "That's a bit freaky finding a body on the beach."

"It is. Nothing smells quite as bad as a decaying human body. Unfortunately, that's not my first one."

"Gross!" she exclaimed, wrinkling her nose.

After a moment, I asked, "What's for dinner tonight?"

"I'm making one of your favorites—braised short ribs. They've been in the oven since we left for the beach."

"I thought something smelled good."

"Yeah, way better than the beach!" she laughed.

After we finished our drinks, Mia returned to the kitchen to check on dinner, and I joined her in the TV room, which was completely open to the kitchen. Anxious to see if there was any news coverage of my beach find, I toggled the remote and sat on the overstuffed leather sofa to watch.

Toward the end of the local stories, I saw the breaking news banner crawl across the bottom of the screen and watched a reporter on Mamaroneck Beach with the police, struggling with her blonde hair as the wind blew strands across her face. She told us, "Although the investigation has yet to begin, I can confirm the body is a white female."

Mia announced that dinner was ready, and I shut off the TV. After choosing a bottle of Cabernet, I eased out the cork, poured two glasses, and held her seat for her. The plates looked marvelous. On each, she had placed two short ribs on a mound of mashed potatoes and drizzled them with Demi-glaze. Alongside were baby carrots. Everything Mia cooked was fantastic. She and her late husband were foodies and vacationed together at European cooking schools.

The kitchen table sat in a bay window with the same view as the living room. With the property gently sloping toward the water, the main floor was elevated at the rear, and a wooden deck ran the length of the house. The beach was just a hundred yards away, and we could see across the Sound to Long Island, a distance of six miles.

While eating and chatting, we watched the boat traffic as the sky turned orange just before sunset. It wasn't long before my mind returned to the body on the beach, my cop-brain clicking in. The fact that it was wrapped and tied in a blanket ruled out an accidental death, so it had to be murder—and by an amateur. A professional killer would have weighed the body down so it could never float to the surface.

Aware of my preoccupation, Mia asked, "What are you thinking about, love?"

"I'm sorry. I guess I was thinking about the body on the beach."

"Yeah, it will take me a while to get over it, too. Are you going to be able to leave it alone?"

"Not my job anymore. I'm sure the police can handle it," I replied.

Mia raised her eyebrows and looked at me with doubting eyes, then grinned. "After we clean up in here, how about we go upstairs and focus on something else?"

Smiling, I leaned closer for a kiss and said, "You'll never get a 'No' from me.

CHAPTER 2

Woken by the sound of my phone vibrating on the nightstand, I reached over, sent the call to voicemail, and snuggled into Mia, not wanting to wake up just yet. A while later, when she rose to brush her teeth, I checked to see who had called so early in the morning. It was the Mamaroneck Police. I listened to the message, pulled on some pants, and went downstairs to make coffee. After a few sips, I returned the call and asked for Detective Preston.

"Homicide, Preston," I heard in an abrupt tone.

"Hello, this is Dan Burnett returning your call."

"Yes, thank you. I understand you're the one who reported the body on the beach yesterday."

"That's right."

"What else can you tell me about it?"

"Nothing, really. I didn't get too close because of the smell. I'm retired NYPD, so I knew what it was and called 911."

"So the body was lying in the surf when you found it?"

"Well, I saw a rolled-up blanket with what I assumed was a body inside."

"Oh, it's definitely a body. Female—white, with no ID. Do you live in the area?"

"My girlfriend lives a little way down the beach."

"Okay, thanks for calling it in."

"Sure, no problem," I said, ending the call.

Mia joined me in the kitchen and hugged me from behind, her head resting on my back. "Good morning, lover. You outdid yourself last night."

"Thank you, sweetheart. I loved every minute of it."

While she poured herself a coffee, I turned on the news to see if there was any new information about the body I discovered on the beach. There was. The same blonde reporter told us, "The body is so decayed that the police will have difficulty identifying it without a DNA match, although there might be enough left of the jaw to use dental records. The detectives wonder if it could be one of the recently reported missing persons."

After breakfast, I asked Mia about her plans for the day.

"I'm taking the train into the city for lunch with one of my fashion designer friends. We haven't seen each other in years."

Mia had a very successful twenty-year career in fashion design before her husband became ill, and I was happy to hear she had stayed in touch with her friends and associates.

I told her about my plans to visit the office and help my partner with some collector car investigations. After dressing, I kissed her goodbye and took my usual route to the office in Scarsdale. Traffic was already congested, primarily due to a backup of cars attempting to enter a Starbucks parking lot. A few moments later, my phone rang, and I smiled when my daughter's face lit up the screen.

"Hi, Hannah."

"Hey, Dad, how are you this morning?" she asked cheerfully.

"All good. What are you up to?"

"Well, I've been interviewing for jobs and have a couple of second interviews lined up. If they offer me a job, I don't know what to say."

"How about *YES*?" I laughed.

"Come on, Dad. You know I've been wrestling with what I want to do."

"I'm sorry, Han. Would you like to meet for lunch and talk about it?"

"I would. Will you be at the office today?"

"I'm heading there now; shall we say 12:30?"

"Perfect. See you then."

Hannah had graduated from Iona University with a bachelor's degree in business finance a few months ago. She was among the top of her class and graduated magna cum laude, so I wasn't surprised to hear she was getting job offers—I was anxious to hear about them.

When I entered the third-floor office in a professional building I shared with my partner Jim Abbott, he was already at his desk working the phones.   The TV was tuned to the local news, showing yesterday's scene on Mamaroneck Beach.

Six months ago, Jim and I solved a case involving two stolen cars—not just any cars, but restored antiques valued at over a million dollars each. Since then, he has kept busy with other collectors, checking for fraud and authenticating vehicles for sale. There was plenty of that work for both of us, and now that the sailing season was winding down, I had the time to pitch in.

Jim, like me, retired from the NYPD. He was just a year older and became a PI a few years ago. He was about my height and weight, and had curly, reddish hair. I always assumed he was Irish, with fair skin, freckles, and light-colored eyes, but never felt the need to ask. He took me under his wing when I retired, helped me get my PI license, and showed me the ropes.

When his call ended, he nodded at the TV and asked, "Wasn't this body on the beach found right near Mia's?"

"Yes. As a matter of fact, I was the one who called it in."

"You're kidding."

"No. We were walking on the beach, and I could smell it a hundred yards away."

"I can imagine—that's a smell you never forget."

"As much as you try," I added.

THE PREVIOUS DAY, Jim had called with a case he thought I'd be interested in and told me about a car theft in Westport, Connecticut. Two masked men in a stolen car followed the owner of an Aston Martin home and roughed him up before driving the car out of his garage while he watched.

After I poured myself a coffee, Jim filled me in on the details and showed me a surveillance video of the whole event from a security camera in the guy's garage. What we witnessed was a typical carjacking, except it happened at the owner's home—very brazen. Jim told me the local police were involved, but the owner wanted a private investigation and could easily afford to hire us.

I started by calling the owner, Michael Lerner, to tell him we would accept the case. After he agreed to our standard fee of $85 per hour plus expenses, he told me more about the theft. "Judging by how they moved, I think they were in their early twenties, and they left behind the car they arrived in. Look, I'm hoping to get the car back before it's chopped up and sold for parts—that's why I'm hiring you."

Speaking in a calm, reasoned tone, he told me the details of the police response. I asked him to email me a few pictures of the car, along with a copy of the title and registration.

My next call was to the Westport Police Department.

"Detective Marks, Please."

"Who's calling?"

"Dan Burnett. I'm a private investigator." After a brief hold, the detective came on the line.

"Mr. Burnett. What can I do for you?"

"Michael Lerner has hired me to find his Aston Martin."

"What, he doesn't think we can handle the case?" he asked.

"I don't know; wealthy people sometimes like to hire their own people."

"We have plenty of those in Westport."

Laughing, I said, "I'm sure you do. Have you made any progress?"

"Well, it's only been a day, but we dusted the stolen car they left behind and only found the owner's prints. We also logged the Aston into the system and put out an APB. That's a recognizable car—I think it will turn up."

"Mr. Lerner hopes it doesn't end up at a chop shop."

"Yeah, that would be a shame," he stated flatly.

"Can we keep each other in the loop on this?"

"Sure. Give me your number."

Jim had overheard my conversation, and when it concluded, he asked, "Does the Police Detective sound competent?"

"I guess so, but they're not going to search every garage in the State of Connecticut."

"True that."

I thought I'd call Wayne Walker, a Connecticut collector car expert who had helped me before. Fortunately, when I called, he answered himself.

"So, Dan, do you have another stolen car you're looking for?"

"I do. I assume you heard about the Aston that got carjacked in Westport?"

"Yeah. Right out of the guy's garage?"

"That's the one. What do you think the thieves would do with that car?"

"Probably just take it for a joy ride," he chuckled.

. "Could they sell it?"

"Someone would be nuts to buy it; you couldn't register it unless they dummy up a title and alter the numbers."

"Have you ever heard of someone holding a car for ransom?"

"I have, but that car was not an antique. It's only worth a hundred grand or so, and the owner can just buy another one with the insurance money."

Smiling at only a hundred grand, I said, "Okay, Wayne. Thanks for your time. Let me know if you hear anything."

"Will do, Dan. Bye now."

After ending the call, Jim offered, "I'll send you the links to all the car auction sites. I use them to confirm the chain of possession, but you could monitor them to see if the thieves try to auction it off."

"Thanks. That might be worth a try."

"Although they might sit on the car for months to let it cool off before trying to sell it," he added.

"I guess I'll just have to be patient and see what happens."

Jim laughed, "Oh yeah, I've seen how good you are with patience!"

CHAPTER 3

Hannah walked in the door a few minutes later, her smile lighting the room. She's tall—5'10", athletic, with long sandy blonde hair and the brightest blue eyes in the world. Today, she was wearing shorts and a polo shirt.

Our office was a single large room with two desks, a conference table, and a comfortable seating cluster consisting of a couch, a couple of tables, and upholstered chairs. Other than a closet and a bathroom along the back wall, that was about it.

"Hello, Hannah!" Jim exclaimed, rising as she approached him for a hug.

"Dad tells me you've become a collector car guru!" she chortled.

"It seems that way."

Hannah will always have a soft spot for Jim, as he was part of the team that rescued her from kidnappers several months ago. After they chatted for a few minutes, Hannah and I left for lunch. It was warm and humid outside, as fall weather had yet to set in, and we walked two buildings over to the Outback Steakhouse. As we entered, the scent of grilled beef piqued our appetites, but once seated, we sensibly ordered two salads topped with grilled chicken. After the waitress poured us water, I asked Hannah about her job search.

"I interviewed with Goldman Sachs a few weeks ago," she said. "The opening was for a bond salesman, and after training, I'd be on the phone all day trying to sell enough to meet a quota. I saw the call center, and it looked like a sweatshop."

"And that didn't appeal to you?" I laughed.

"No way! Too much pressure among sharks."

"And the others?"

As the displeasure on her face turned to a smile, she said, "I interviewed with Chase Bank for executive assistant training. It was a way more appealing environment, and I'd be in the executive office with all the bigwigs."

Nodding, I said, "That sounds good. I hear their CEO is one of the smartest guys around."

"I think I'm leaning that way, but I went on another interview yesterday with a start-up company that developed a new accounting software. I'd be doing outside sales, and after the IPO, the stock bonus could be worth a hundred thousand dollars."

"That's exciting, but what if the IPO never happens?"

"They made it sound like a sure thing."

"I'm sure they did. I recommend you do some research before counting on that," I added, trying to protect her from the hype of the business world.

"You're probably right," her spirit diminished.

"Hey, I don't mean to sound negative; I'm just saying check them out."

"I get it. Thanks for being my sounding board."

"How are things at home with your mom?"

"Great. Living there for the last few months has taken a lot of pressure off me. One of these days, I'll look for a place of my own."

This past spring, with one month remaining in her senior year at Iona University, Hannah was kidnapped by some bad cops I was investigating. With the help of Jim and a few friends, we rescued her in a military-style raid that left two of the cops dead. It was a traumatic experience for her, and I'm sure moving back home has been comforting. She's also been seeing a therapist.

When our food arrived, we continued chatting about her prospects. I tried to steer the conversation toward what she would enjoy doing, rather than the initial paycheck. While I could certainly understand anyone's desire for more money, I knew that having a fulfilling job you enjoyed doing was equally important, if not more so. After finishing lunch, we returned to the office parking lot, where we hugged before she drove away. My eyes followed as she exited the lot, wondering where her teenage years had gone—they seemed more like hours.

Back in the office, Jim said, "Hannah looks like she's doing well, all things considered."

"Yeah, I'm really proud of her. The therapist has helped her a lot."

"How was your lunch?"

"We just walked over to Outback. She's interviewing for jobs and wanted to bounce a few off me."

"Let me guess: you two went to a steakhouse and just had a salad," he quipped.

Smiling back at him, I admitted, "You have us pegged, Jim."

"I'm sure she'll have no problems finding a job. Magna cum laude and all that."

"It sounds like she'll be getting a few offers."

"Good to hear."

"If you have nothing more for me today, I think I'll shove off."

"We're good; I appreciate you taking that Westport case off my plate. Let me know how you do."

"Okay, buddy," I said as I walked out the door.

MIA WAS STILL out when I returned to the house. I set my laptop on the dining room table, which had become my workspace. The dining room was located at the front of the house, alongside a two-story foyer and staircase, with her library on the opposite side. Once the laptop booted, I perused the links Jim had sent me for the auction sites. I had no illusions of finding the Aston this soon—I just wanted to familiarize myself with the sites.

A couple of hours later, looking out the front window, I saw Mia's Mercedes SUV pull into the driveway and disappear into the garage. I closed my laptop and went to greet her as she entered the house. "Hi, sweetheart. How was your day in the Big Apple?"

After rising on her toes for a kiss, she said, "How about you make us a drink, and I'll tell you all about it," she replied energetically.

"Sure. It is about that time, isn't it? What's your choice today?"

"How about one of your martinis?"

"You got it."

As she set down her things and removed her heels, I shook up a batch of slightly dirty Ketel One Martinis and strained them into the appropriate glasses. After adding a blue cheese-stuffed olive, we touched glasses before taking the first sip.

While sitting on the TV room couch, Mia continued, "So, my friend Sandy, whom I love, has started her own design house and wants me to partner with her."

"Whoa, I didn't know you were considering returning to work."

"I wasn't, but this sounds exciting. She just signed a contract with a high-end apparel manufacturer to design couture evening wear, which is exactly what we worked together on for years."

I could read the excitement on her face, her eyes bright and wide.

"What is couture evening wear?"

"Expensive!" she laughed. "Couture means limited production and original designs. Wealthy women wouldn't be caught dead at an event in something off the rack. If two people showed up wearing the same dress, they'd be horrified."

"I think I understand. What did you tell her?"

"I told her I needed a few days to think about it."

"What does your tummy tell you?"

"It's tempting. I'm already designing things in my mind."

"I can tell you're excited. You know I'll support whatever you want to do."

"Thanks, love." After another quick kiss, she said, "How was your day?"

"I helped Jim with a stolen car case and had lunch with Hannah."

"How's she doing?"

"I think she's doing quite well. While I can't know what's going on inside her head, I no longer see signs of trauma. She's been interviewing and wanted to talk to me about job offers."

"Oh, that's so good to hear. Is she still seeing the therapist?" Mia asked.

"Yeah, she's going every week."

"She should—that was quite an ordeal. I'd be curled up in a ball somewhere in the corner of a room!"

"It was good to see her today."

"I'll bet." After a pause, she asked, "How does Pad Thai sound tonight? I found a recipe I think we might like."

"Sounds good to me."

"All right. I'm going to change before cooking."

As she went upstairs, I took our empty glasses into the kitchen and turned on the local news. Before long, the coverage turned to the body on the beach. They reported that it had been identified through a DNA match as a twenty-two-year-old woman who had been reported missing in Riverdale a month ago. Her name was Natalie Morgan, and they showed a few pictures of her. In one, she was wearing a cap and gown, and I immediately thought of Hannah, who'd worn a cap and gown just a few months ago. The mental image rattled me—a young woman, fresh out of school with her whole life ahead of her. It reminded me how cruel this world can be.

Mia returned to the kitchen wearing yoga pants and a Foo Fighters T-shirt. After digging out a wok from a lower cabinet, she chopped and prepared the ingredients and warned me that it would cook quickly once it hit the pan. I told her I was ready and opened a couple of cold Heinekens. Within a few minutes, she set plates mounded with Pad Thai on the table, then topped them with chopped peanuts. It was fantastic, with just the right amount of spice. Over dinner, I told her about the body being identified, and she thought she remembered reports of the woman's disappearance.

Later, in our happy place, she led a discussion of the pros and cons of returning to work. It had completely consumed her.

CHAPTER 4

While enjoying my morning coffee, I turned on the TV to see the latest on the body I'd discovered. I began to imagine how I would handle the investigation if I were still a cop and it was assigned to me, further spurring my interest. That morning, the media showed an interview with Natalie Morgan's parents after they had confirmed the identity of the body. Her mother was crying while her father comforted his wife. I knew how tough that must have been, especially considering the body's condition—it always amazed me that families would agree to interviews when it was the last thing they needed.

The station had prepared a video package of Natalie, featuring her as a young girl playing soccer, then in high school as a cheerleader, and finally graduating from Hunter College with a nursing degree. They ran this loop repeatedly while covering the story. They also had taped interviews with coworkers who were in tears. I learned she had grown up in Riverdale and was a nurse at Westchester Medical Center. There were no clues as to the cause of her disappearance, and she was last seen leaving work at the end of her shift—nothing out of the ordinary, and not much for the police detectives to go on.

Mia joined me for our usual breakfast of berries and yogurt, but she was quiet and preoccupied—I assumed about returning to work. I went upstairs to get dressed, and when I came back down, Mia was in her library setting up an easel with a drawing board.

"What are you doing, sweetheart?" I asked.

"I thought I'd try sketching to see if I still can."

"Wouldn't it be like riding a bike?"

She chuckled. "I have no idea. We'll see."

"Good luck with it. I'm heading to the marina."

"Okay, enjoy your day."

On my way to City Island, the AC was cranking, and it took everything my Jeep Grand Cherokee had to combat the heat and humidity as the sun broiled the windshield. When I heard my phone's ringtone, I lowered the AC so I could hear.

"Hello," I answered.

"Hi Dan, It's Willy."

"Hey, bud. I haven't heard from you in a while."

Willy Grant was an NYPD Detective out of the 50th Precinct in Riverdale.

"I know; I hear you found the body in Mamaroneck?"

"That's right. But I didn't get very close; the smell was awful."

"I'll bet. The Natalie Morgan case is mine."

"No shit! What a coincidence."

"Yeah, Bella and I were assigned when Natalie was first reported missing. We hoped she had just run off with a boyfriend. Certainly not this."

"Do you have anything to work with?" I asked, hoping for some inside information.

"Nothing. No clothing, no jewelry—just a body, or what was left of it."

"I'm sorry; I wish I had something to help you."

"I didn't think you would, but I figured I'd call anyway."

"I'm glad you did. It's good to hear your voice."

"Yours too. Take it easy, Dan."

Willy and I had worked together in the past; the last time was on Mia's brother's murder case. He's a large Black man in great shape. Willy and his partner, Bella Fratelli, watch what they eat and pump iron every day before work. They are both ripped, and whenever I saw them, I felt guilty for no longer hitting the gym.

City Island sits just off the mainland of Pelham, New York. After crossing a short causeway, it's less than two miles long with just one road that dead-ends in a turnaround. Along that road are dozens of seafood restaurants and marinas. That's about it; a bit honky-tonk, but a perfect place for keeping a boat.

When I reached the marina, I wandered down the ramp to "A" dock and stepped aboard the transom of my sailboat, *Privateer*. My dock neighbor, Vinnie, had his pedestal apart, with wires spread out all over the place. We chatted for a few minutes before I went below, welcomed by the familiar scent of fiberglass and varnished teak. I found my to-do list on the chart table and looked for a task I felt like doing today.

There is always work to be done on a sailboat—a repair, some maintenance, or something that needs cleaning. I focused on end-of-season chores like changing the engine oil, checking the antifreeze, and topping off the batteries; there would be more to do before hauling her out for the winter. Previously, I had kept her in the water all winter because I lived aboard. But this year, feeling confident in our relationship, I planned to stay at Mia's.

WHEN I RETURNED to her house, I found her in the library, standing before her drawing board with large sheets of sketching paper taped to the walls and others strewn about the room. Each sheet had a sketch of a faceless woman in a dress, all of them different. After a kiss, I lingered over her shoulder to see what she was working on. The dress she drew had sharp, exaggerated shoulders that tapered to almost nothing at the waist. Every feature appeared exaggerated, and I was amazed at how she drew creases and folds in the fabric—it seemed the figure was in motion, twirling around.

"How's it going?" I asked.

Smiling, she said, "Pretty good. I can still translate what I envision onto paper."

"I had no idea you were such an artist."

"This is what I needed to see. I was afraid I'd lost it."

"Looks good to me," I offered.

"It is good, love. I'm unsure of the styles, but I can still sketch!"

"Does this mean you're going to work with Sandy?"

"I don't know yet," she laughed, "but this was one hurdle I had to overcome."

With my arms around Mia's waist, I hugged her from behind, kissing her neck and catching a hint of her scent. "I'm happy for you."

"I'm going to pick up in here and then go up and bathe. I haven't even thought about dinner."

"How about we go out?"

"That sounds nice. You pick the place."

"Okay, I'll have a beverage waiting for you when you come down."

"Thanks, love."

I left her to pick up and went to the kitchen table with my laptop to check emails. Finishing quickly, I searched for local restaurants to have dinner. I came across a new one, Crawfords, in Larchmont, just a few minutes away. I made a reservation online, then remembered the cocktail I had promised. After filling the shaker with crushed ice, I poured the ingredients for a Martini and began shaking. I heard Mia descend the stairs as I dropped the olives in martini glasses, and had just finished pouring when she appeared beside me.

"Cheers," I said as we touched glasses. She was wearing a sleeveless knit dress that fit her perfectly. Her youthful, toned body looked great in anything she wore, and when I caught a hint of her scent, romantic thoughts dashed through my head. While Mia never smelled of perfume, the scent just seemed to be hers, something I noticed the first time we met. It wasn't flowery or sweet; perhaps mysterious would be the best description. There was always just a hint, and I couldn't get enough of it.

"I made a reservation at Crawfords for 6:30. How does that sound to you?" I asked.

"Oh, that's the new place I've heard about. I'd love to try it."

We took our drinks out on the deck and gazed across the sound, something we never seem to tire of. I told her about Willy Grant's assignment to the Natalie Morgan case, knowing she thought fondly of him for helping solve her brother's murder.

"So you spoke with Willy?"

"Yes, just today. He doesn't have much to work with yet."

"Maybe he needs your help again," she teased.

"Haha. I doubt that."

We watched a classic schooner sailing in the distance. Its beautiful lines were a reminder of yachting's glory days of custom Herreshoff designs. Oil barons and industrialists of extreme wealth commissioned them over a century ago, and being a sucker for sailing history, whenever I saw yachts like this, my imagination took me back in time to the days when the Liptons and Vanderbilts raced across the Atlantic for the pride of their nations.

MIA AND I were seated by the front window in the restaurant overlooking the sidewalk—great for people-watching. The restaurant's interior had been completely redone in black and white, with soft lighting, and the scent of fresh paint lingered in the air. After the waiter poured us water, we perused the menu and saw a variety of steaks, chops, and seafood; they referred to themselves as purveyors of American cuisine. Eyeing the dishes being served to other tables, we chose veal chops with Marsala mushrooms, a Caesar salad for two, and a side of garlicky spinach. Paired with a bottle of California Cabernet.

Over dinner, I asked Mia to tell me more about the fashion design business.

"It's fast-paced. Trends come and go, and when a look becomes hot, everyone tries to put their spin on it," she said. "In the couture business, we're not designing for the masses but for the wealthy. It's not unusual for a dress to cost five thousand dollars."

Shocked, my eyes opened wide, and I said, "I can't imagine a dress costing that much."

"It's not something you wear every day. It's for special occasions, like a ball or an opera, never to be worn again. At least not in the same country!" she laughed. "They dress to impress."

"I'm not sure I'd be impressed. I probably couldn't tell the difference between one dress and another, just the difference between the women wearing them."

"I'm sure that's true, but wealthy women can tell you the designer's name the moment they see the dress," Mia smiled.

"Amazing. There's a whole world out there I know nothing about."

"Don't feel bad; we're only talking about the top tenth of one percent."

We both enjoyed our meals, and by the time we finished, the restaurant was packed. It had become increasingly noisy, so we hurried to pay and left.

After returning to Mia's house, we secured everything and went upstairs, where I took a quick shower. When I came out and saw just the flickering light of candles, I knew our evening would get even better.

CHAPTER 5

"Another body found on the beach" was the headline on the morning news while I waited for the coffee to finish brewing. After pouring a cup, I sat down to watch. The reporter and camera were set up on Sands Point Beach, Long Island, directly across the Sound and just a few miles from Mamaroneck, as the crow flies. It was the same blonde reporter we saw last week, although her hair wasn't blowing across her face this early in the day. Her name was Elsa Nordstrom.

They ran a loop of recorded video of the police and first responders. I watched as they dragged a rolled-up rug out of the water, using a quad ATV with big tires just after sunrise. Again, the seagulls were circling, their caws drowning out the sound of the ATV. When the image returned to the live reporter, she told us the body in the rug was an adult, white female that had been in the water for quite some time, similar to the body found in Mamaroneck. She speculated that the events were related and were the acts of a serial killer. After viewing the video loop several times, my interest was piqued, and I wondered if that might indeed be the case.

Mia entered the kitchen, poured herself a coffee, and sat beside me. "Good morning, lover."

"Good morning, sweetheart. You're going to want to see the breaking news."

"What is it?"

"You'll see."

She looked at me, slightly perturbed that I wouldn't just tell her, but sat silently, sipping coffee while waiting for the news to resume. When the commercials were over, they returned to the reporter on the beach.

"Oh my God, another one?" Mia blurted.

"Yup. On Sand Point Beach, directly across the Sound."

"Do we have a serial killer?"

"It's possible. The reporter is speculating we do."

"Do you remember the Son of Sam murders? That went on for months."

"I remember it well. The entire NYPD worked on that. We should know if that's the case as soon as they identify the body."

After we had each contemplated the news, I rose to refill my coffee and asked, "What are your plans today?"

"I promised Sandy I'd call her today. We'll see where that leads."

"I think I'll hang around here today and do some research on the computer."

She stood, smiled, and said, "Just a couple of homebodies!"

"Yup." I hugged her, and she went up on her toes and kissed me on the cheek.

After breakfast, Mia busied herself in her library while I set up in the dining room with my laptop and notepad. My mission for the day was to learn as much as I could from the car auction websites. There were a few of them, and each had its own format. I tried searching for

Aston Martins and only found a few. Some sites allowed me to narrow the search by year, transmission type, body style, and color. Over the remainder of the morning, I searched for Astons with the details for Richard Lerner's car. Most sites allowed me to save the search and receive notifications if any matching vehicles became available in the future. Perfect!

When I finished, it was lunchtime, so I warmed up some leftover Pad Thai for Mia and me. While eating, she told me she was getting serious about returning to work.

"The more I think about it, the more my juices begin flowing again," she said. "Sandy believes we only need to work in the office a few days a week, and we can collaborate from home on our computers. I might need to get a more sophisticated printer, though."

As I watched her, I saw the excitement in her body language. It was clear that her "juices were flowing," as she said, and I knew then that Mia would return to work. I was thrilled for her, but wondered how it would affect our relationship—everything was so perfect the way it was. Time would tell.

I spent the rest of the day on the boat, not accomplishing much, other than staying out of Mia's hair. She had lived alone for a few years before I came along, and I thought she might like some space while figuring out her career.

I managed to finish a few things on the list, but the rest would have to wait until we were done sailing for the season.

When I returned, Mia was energized and dancing around the kitchen with AirPods in her ears as she prepared a big chef's salad for dinner. When she noticed me, she removed them and gave me a peck on the cheek.

"Would you like a cocktail this evening?" I asked.

"No thanks. I'm working on cranberry juice. Would you like one?

"Sure, I'll get it."

I guessed we were eating healthy tonight, which was fine by me. I could use a night off from high-calorie meals and alcohol. The salad was delicious; most of the ingredients were from her garden, and she topped it with grilled shrimp.

I was up first and began my routine of watching the news with my morning coffee. The washed-up bodies were still the lead story, and we were told of a DNA match for the second woman. Her name was Laura Kelly, and she was first reported missing nearly two months ago. She, too, was a nurse and was last seen leaving work at a doctor's office in Croton-on-Hudson. As they did with Natalie Morgan, the network had prepared a video package to run on a continuous loop. They showed Laura growing up in Dobbs Ferry, where she was a member of the high school soccer team, and pictures of her mugging for the camera with her friends and siblings.

For the first time, the media used the phrase "The Nurse Murders." While I agreed that theory was likely, I thought substantiating it would take a third victim. My detective's brain began clicking, and I wondered why both bodies were found in Long Island Sound, even though the women lived and worked in different places.

I started thinking about the questions that needed answers. Were the women held captive and their bodies dumped later from the same place? Were there river currents around New York City that would cause the bodies to wash up in a similar area? They were reported missing a month apart; why did they wash up just days apart? Mia interrupted my thoughts before I got further into it.

"Good morning, love."

"Good morning, sweetheart."

While pouring her coffee, she noticed what I was watching and sat beside me to hear the whole story.

"Nurse Murders?" she said at the next commercial.

"That's what they're calling it."

"What do we have, some sicko with a nurse fetish on the loose?"

"Sounds like it."

"Lord help us; there's always something."

I shook my head, remembering how the media could create a frenzy around events like this.

Mia asked, "What are you thinking?"

"Oh, just about trying to do police work during a media frenzy. Sometimes, it can be helpful, but usually, it makes it more difficult."

"I can only imagine."

When the station came back from commercial, they announced that a special report would air that evening on Natalie Morgan and Laura Kelly. They told us the report would be in-depth and anchored by Elsa Nordstrom.

As they moved on to other news, Mia asked, "Do you have plans today?"

"Not really. If nothing better comes up, I'll work at the office. How about you?"

"I was thinking of taking the day off. I've been obsessing over this work thing, and I want to clear my head and see how I feel in a day. How about we go sailing?"

"Something better just came up!" I laughed.

She kissed me on the cheek and rose to make breakfast.

The wind was light as we left the dock. We motored into the Sound, hoping the wind would pick up when we were further away from land. It increased enough to fill the sails, but it was clear we weren't going anywhere today. We made our best speed heading due east on a beam reach. With the autopilot steering and the sun shining bright, we lounged around the cockpit, catching rays that might be our last of the season.

Mia was wearing a little black string bikini that barely covered anything, which, I must admit, gave me a place to rest my eyes all afternoon. The only time she wears it is out here on the boat with no one else around. She'd wear a traditional one-piece anywhere else to avoid drawing attention to herself.

While Mia was the sexiest woman on the planet, it was a side of her that she only shared with me. The rest of the time, she dressed comfortably or conservatively, and you'd have to look closely to notice her flawless beauty. This style of hers is what drew me to her initially, and what caused me difficulty while working on her brother's murder. I felt like I had discovered something only visible to me. I asked her about it once, and she told me she learned early in her career that men—and a few women—leered at her as an object and didn't take her seriously. Since then, it had become her style.

CHAPTER 6

That evening, after dinner, we watched the special report on the two murdered nurses. The opening scene featured a video of a young Natalie Morgan running through a sprinkler in the backyard of her childhood home with her friends. All the children were acting silly and having fun without a care in the world.

Elsa's voice narrated over the footage, recounting a fairytale story about Natalie's youth. The next several minutes illustrated how she was just like every other girl in America, sharing the same dreams and aspirations. Some of the video repeated what had been shown immediately after the discovery of her body, but this report delved deeper, featuring interviews with her friends and family.

We once again saw her parents, Cindy and Doug Morgan, in tears as they spoke about the loss of their daughter. When her father managed to say, "Natalie was the center of my universe," my stomach clenched, my mind leaped to Hannah, understanding exactly how he felt.   Another interview featured one of her childhood friends, now grown, who had appeared in the opening scene running through the sprinkler. We followed Natalie as she grew up wearing braces, then as a cheerleader, and finally witnessed her high school and nursing school graduations. The piece concluded with interviews of her fellow nurses, all expressing their disbelief that she was truly gone.

After the commercial break, the special report continued with Laura Kelly. Once again, Elsa spoke over the footage of a young girl in pigtails playing soccer, first with the kids from the neighborhood and then as a team member with other girls. In many of the clips, she was aware of the camera and stuck out her tongue or wiggled her fingers with her thumbs in her ears, and we heard her giggling. We also saw her playing other sports: field hockey, volleyball, and softball. In later years, we saw her playing soccer competitively with her high school team. The pigtails were gone, replaced by a ponytail, and Elsa told us she was the team captain. Again, we saw interviews with her parents and friends, just as heartfelt as with the Morgans. The segment concluded with images of Laura at work in a doctor's office wearing a white nurse's uniform.

While Elsa's report mainly celebrated these girls' lives, I knew from experience that the audience would be left wondering who would be next.

THE NEXT DAY, Mia officially decided to work with Sandy at their new fashion design house—no surprise to me. She would work from home most days and take the train into the city twice a week, depending on the project. Her first day would be Monday; needless to say, she was psyched and back to dancing in the kitchen while preparing meals.

Hannah called one evening, sounding thrilled, and told me she had taken the job with Chase Bank. I was delighted for her, having hoped that would be her choice. She would be starting work on

Monday, and we planned to get together the following weekend so I could hear all about her first week on the job.

With the two women in my life now gainfully employed, I felt I needed to get up and out of the house, too. So, on Monday, I went into the office and worked on more collector car assignments. Jim taught me how to create an "abstract of title" for cars that our customers considered purchasing. An abstract of title was a fancy term for a history of ownership. He showed me how to find the manufacturer's certificate of origin and access state registration records. It was pretty straightforward, except for the age of some of these vehicles. The older they were, the more challenging it was to locate the documents. If built before World War I, they may not exist at all. Once I'd done a few abstracts, I became reasonably proficient.

Of course, as ex-cops, we discussed the nurse murders daily. We scoured the news for bits of information and speculated on theories. For us, it was just curiosity and exercising our minds. However, there were two other reported cases of missing persons over the last few months. Both were nurses, and both had yet to be found.

"How long do you think it will be until another body turns up in the Sound?" Jim asked.

"My guess is within a couple of weeks, but can you imagine what it's like for these young women's families?"

"They must be afraid to turn on the news," Jim replied.

LIFE WITH MIA had not changed during her first week of work. She was home most days, and when she went into the city, she was always home before dinner. She seemed as happy as always, if not more so. I guessed she had missed the sense of productivity and accomplishment after all. In the evenings, I was eager to hear about her day, and she would tell me about the projects she was working on. While I didn't understand the fashion-related terms, I could sense her enthusiasm and couldn't have been happier for her.

On Friday evening, anxious to hear about her new job, I called Hannah to schedule a time for us to have dinner.

"Hey, Dad."

"Well, how was it?"

"Great. Everyone is so nice to me. There's a lot to learn, but my education relates to all of it. I think it's going to work out."

Sensing the enthusiasm in her voice, I said, "Good to hear, Han. Do you have an evening open for dinner?"

"Sure, tomorrow works for me. I'd like to see Mia too, if she's up for it."

"I'll invite her. Do you have a place in mind?"

"Nope. You pick."

"Okay, I'll call you tomorrow with a place."

"I'm looking forward to seeing you two."

"Bye, Han. Love you!"

"Love you, too, Dad!"

After ending the call, I asked Mia if she'd like to go to dinner with Hannah and me the next day.

"Sure. I'd like to hear about her new job. Where are we going?"

"I don't know yet. Let me check the weather; maybe we'll meet on the boat." I scrolled through the weather app on my phone and saw that there would be thunderstorms in the afternoon.

"Rain tomorrow. City Island would be a zoo on Saturday anyhow."

"What does she like?"

"She likes Giuseppe's and pizza with burnt crust," I laughed.

"I'm not sure pizza is the best way to celebrate her new job, but I've never been to Giuseppe's."

"You might like it. It's standard family-style Italian—I've taken her there since childhood. We can think on it and let her know tomorrow."

MIA SPENT SATURDAY morning in her garden. It was harvest time, and everything seemed to ripen simultaneously. As she picked what was ready, I hauled it into the house in baskets and piled it on the kitchen counter. There was zucchini, peppers, cucumbers, lettuce, and lots of tomatoes. She planned to jar the tomatoes for use over the winter.

Hearing distant thunder, Mia came inside when the sky darkened and began sorting through the items, deciding what to eat, what to jar, and what to give away. While she was doing that, I asked if she had any more thoughts on a restaurant for tonight.

"Let's go to Giuseppe's. I've heard you talk about it, so I'd like to try it."

"Good, it's in New-Ro and will be a short drive for Hannah in this weather."

I CALLED GIUSEPPE'S and spoke with his wife, Bianca. She said 7:00 would be a good time and looked forward to seeing us. Then I texted Hannah, suggesting we meet her there.

Dressed casually, we drove to New Rochelle in light rain. After parking, we were greeted by the aroma of roasted garlic, even twenty feet from the front door. We were a few minutes early, and Bianca rushed over to greet us as soon as we walked inside.

Expecting Hannah, Bianca said, "And who do we have here?"

"This is Mia. Hannah will be joining us shortly."

Bianca briefly looked Mia up and down, then smiled at me, nodding her approval. She sat us at our usual window table, laid out three menus, and took my order for a bottle of Chianti.

While Bianca retrieved the wine, Mia raised her eyebrows and said, "What was that all about?"

"It means she approves of you," I said with a smile.

"That's good to know!" Mia laughed.

Just then, Hannah walked in the door and spotted us. I rose for a hug and helped her off with her jacket. She and Mia hugged, and Bianca rushed over to greet her. Bianca poured our wine, then scurried off to welcome some new patrons coming through the door.

Giuseppe's hadn't changed a bit in all the years we've been coming here. There was the same mural of the Bay of Naples on one wall and the same shelves of Chianti bottles on another. Bianca hadn't changed either, besides the addition of thin-rimmed glasses. As always, she didn't carry an order pad—she remembered everything.

After our first sips of wine, Mia handed Hannah a grocery bag with handles and said, "Here are some things from my garden—just picked today. I hope you like vegetables because I can keep you supplied for a month!"

Hannah took a peek inside and said, "I love veggies, especially homegrown! Thank you."

Mia perused her menu and asked, "What do you recommend?"

"I always get the lasagna, but everything's good here," Hannah replied.

There was no reason for Hannah or me to open our menus.

I said, "So, tell us about your first week at Chase Bank."

And that she did. Hannah told us about all the people there and what she was doing. Mia asked questions, and Hannah eagerly answered. When Bianca saw us in deep discussion, she dropped off a basket of garlic bread without interrupting. I just listened as Hannah and Mia continued talking. They were bonding, and I was happy to witness it.

Eventually, we ordered, with Mia joining Hannah with the lasagna. I ordered my usual linguine with red clam sauce and a family-style Italian salad for the table. As the conversation continued, I could barely get a word in edgewise.

When our entrées arrived, Bianca refilled our water glasses and kept the basket of garlic bread full. We had a wonderful time, and when we finished, Mia praised the food while Hannah and I just nodded.

"I have a lasagna recipe I'd like you to try, Hannah. How about coming for dinner some night?" Mia asked.

"I'd love to. I'd also like to see your house; Dad has told me all about it."

"Great, we'll do that soon."

We remained at the table for a while, sipping espresso sweetened with anisette. When we were the last people left, I paid the tab as Bianca fussed over Hannah on the way out.

On the way home, Mia said, "I love your daughter. She reminds me of myself when I was twenty-one, full of energy and excited about the future. And those eyes are captivating!"

"Thanks, sweetheart. I'm happy to see you two get along so well."

"It's more than that, Dan," she said as she hugged my arm and rested her head on my shoulder.

ON MONDAY, IT was back to work for both of us. As I drove to the office, there was breaking news on the radio. Another body had been found, this time floating among the docks at a marina in Mamaroneck. The report stated that it was another white female, badly decayed, like the previous two. Unlike the others, though, this one wasn't wrapped at all. I knew a human body in the water would initially float for a few hours and then sink. After weeks in the water, it would bloat and return to the surface.

When I arrived at the office, Jim was watching the news report on television. Besides the lack of being wrapped in a rug or blanket, it seemed like the same M.O.

"Looks like you were right, Dan—less than a week."

"This is one time I wish I weren't right, but it confirms we have a serial killer out there."

"That it does. I wonder which missing woman it is."

"We'll know soon enough. I'm sure the families are on pins and needles."

With the media also confident that it would be one of the nurses, it didn't take long to become the primary topic of conversation in the greater New York area.

Jim and I spent the rest of the day at our desks researching collector cars. By mid-afternoon, we were completely caught up with the backlog. As I was leaving for the day, I told him I might not be coming into the office until he needed me. As Jim weighed the thought, I noticed he tipped his head to the right side to crack his neck. It was something I'd seen him do before.

MIA HAD THE local news on when I entered the house. After a quick kiss, I sat beside her and watched as Elsa Nordstrom stood on the dock and told us that, yes, it was another nurse. Her name was Sierra Swan from Stamford, Connecticut, and she was one of the previously reported nurses, missing since August 15th. She had been employed as a renal dialysis nurse at White Plains Hospital. So far, they were all white, female nurses between the ages of twenty-one and twenty-five, and had all been last seen leaving work.

Mia said, "I guess that confirms we have a nurse murderer."

"That it does. Every young nurse in the area should be on alert."

"Will it be easy to profile this guy?"

"Well, there's still a possibility that it's not a guy. However, many men have a thing for women in uniform. I'm sure the police are already looking into anyone with a criminal history involving nurses in uniform."

Wanting to change the topic, I reached for her hand and said, "So, tell me about your day, sweetheart."

"Jen and I are collaborating on a one-off design for a doctor's wife. It's a custom order for her to wear to a leukemia research fundraiser in November."

"Wouldn't she be better off giving the money to the Leukemia Society?"

Mia laughed, "I'm sure it's a worthy cause, but I'd rather she pay us for the dress!"

I smiled, "I can understand that."

"By the way, we're having pasta primavera tonight—I've got to use up these veggies."

Like everything she makes, the pasta was delicious. After dinner, we returned to our happy place with cups of decaf coffee and a small plate of dark chocolate. Looking out over the water, we gazed at pinpoints of light on the dark horizon and tried to decipher which were on land and which were on water.

After a few sips of coffee, Mia stretched out with her head on my lap, nibbling a piece of chocolate. We talked about going sailing again before the season ended while I idly stroked her hair. I began lightly caressing her forehead, and when she closed her eyes, my fingertips brushed over her eyebrows and eyelids. Before long, my caress moved to her earlobes and neck, causing her to purr.

I lingered there for several minutes, our conversation ending as Mia focused on my touch. When my caress wandered to her breasts, her breath quickened, and I could sense her arousal. She quietly rose and led me up the curved staircase to her bedroom. After removing our clothes, we stepped into her marble and glass-walled shower, carefully washed each other, and began kissing under the streaming water, sucking on each other's lips as the water poured down our faces. After toweling each other dry, we climbed into her big bed and made love for the rest of the evening.

Making love with Mia was an extraordinary experience. Sometimes, she had an initial hunger that had to be fulfilled before she could relax and savor the joys of intimacy. I'd like to think this was born out of passion for me, but I had no way to know for sure. Once she got past that immediate need, Mia became the most tender, imaginative lover possible and could remain in an amorous state for hours. It was during these intimate times that we truly bonded.

CHAPTER 7

The following day, I returned to the car auction websites to search for Aston Martins. An hour into it, I saw one of the large, televised auction companies had recently consigned a car resembling Michael Lerner's, and I emailed him a link to the listing. Twenty minutes later, he called.

"Hi, Dan. That does look like my car. The listing says the auction will be in West Palm?"

"That's right, this coming weekend. I can inquire about the car for more details, pictures, etc."

"Do that, please. The colors are right, and with more pictures, I can pick out little details that might rule it in or out."

"I'll get on that today and let you know what I find out."

"Thanks, Dan."

I MADE AN online inquiry about the car through the auction company's website and requested a photo of the VIN, pictures of the tires, and anything else available. An hour later, I had their response.

I immediately noticed that the VIN in the photo did not match the number on Michael's title, but the VIN photo matched the title and other paper documents they had included. Other images showed the interior from various angles, and close-ups of the tires focused on the brand, size, and tread depth. After forwarding everything to Michael, I recalled a discussion I had with Wayne Walker a few months prior, when he'd told me about counterfeit cars. He had described how it was done with fraudulent titles and numbers stamped on the chassis, engine, and other manufacturer-chosen places. I returned to the various websites that showed pictures of the VIN for all the cars listed and searched for other Aston Martins.

Like most manufacturers, this one placed a metal placard just inside the bottom of the windshield and a sticker on the driver's side door jamb. I examined the VIN for each car closely and noticed that the placard was attached with rivets. Looking back at the pictures I was emailed, I saw that the placard appeared to be glued or bonded in some way, with no visible rivets. Needing help understanding this irregularity, I forwarded everything to Jim and asked him to call when he had a chance to look at the photos. A few minutes later, he did.

"Hi, Dan. What should I be looking for in the photos?"

"Look at the VIN placards; see how most are riveted, but one has no rivets?"

A few moments later, he said, "I do. I also see that the numbers are in a slightly different font. See how the numeral 1 differs from the ones with rivets?"

"Yes. Do you think it's a fake VIN?"

"Let me do a little tracking of this vehicle's history. I'll get back to you this afternoon."

"Thanks."

Shortly after speaking with Jim, Michael called. "Hi, Dan. I see nothing that would rule this out as my car. I'd recently put new tires on it, which were the same Michelin model as the ones in the pictures. The original tires were Pirelli's."

"Interesting. My partner is researching the history of the VIN as we speak," I said.

"Do one of us need to go to the auction and claim the car as stolen?"

"Perhaps. If we find some questionable title history, I assume the auction company would go to great lengths to protect their reputation and make it right."

"Looking at my calendar, I'm supposed to be in Bermuda this weekend with my wife. Are you available to go to Florida?" he asked.

"I am, but let's see what Jim comes up with first."

"Okay," he said.

"I'll keep you posted."

AN HOUR LATER, I heard back from Jim. "Hi, Dan. I traced the VIN to a track car wrecked at Sebring last year. I just spoke to the previous owner in Florida. He told me that after having the car on the road for two years, he modified it for track use and let the registration expire. Last year, he rolled it over while racing, and it was deemed a total loss. He sold it to a salvage company for a few grand and assumed they sold off the parts."

"This might be our car, then," I said.

"It very well could be. When is the auction?"

"This coming weekend, in Florida."

"I suggest you call the auction company and tell them they might have a fraudulent consignment," Jim said.

"Wouldn't they just refuse to accept the car, and that would be the end of it?"

"I see where you're going here. Our client wants the car back, and you'd like to repossess it at the show."

"Something like that, what do you think?"

"I still think you should call the auction company. Don't identify the car until you know what they're willing to do."

"Okay. I'll do that now. Thanks."

When I called the auction company, I asked to speak to someone about a possible fraudulent car listed for the West Palm auction. I was told I would need to speak with one of the owners, but they were both gone for the day. I left my name and number, and they said one of them would call me the following day.

Barry Johnson, one of the auction company's owners, called me the following morning. I explained the reason for yesterday's call and asked about their policy toward fraudulently titled cars.

"Well, Mr. Burnett, we cooperate with all law enforcement and certainly don't want to auction off illegitimate or stolen cars. I'm assuming you want to know the car's whereabouts."

"That's correct. If I identify the car, you're not obligated to locate it for me, are you?"

"Contractually, no, but we do want to maintain our reputation. Here's what I suggest you do: Let the car come into the auction site this week. It will then be in our possession, and we can lock it up pending a legal order."

"Would you recommend I show up in person?"

"That would be best. We have knowledgeable staff on hand who can assist you in locating your identification numbers. If you tell me which car it is, I can confirm when it arrives."

I felt there was no longer a reason to conceal the car's identity, so I shared the details and the consignment number with him. I heard the clicking of a keyboard, and then he said, "That car is scheduled to arrive today. When it's logged in, I'll call you back."

"Thanks, Barry. I look forward to hearing from you."

"Sure, happy to help."

Assuming I would be flying to Florida in the next few days, I called Michael Lerner, told him my plans, and asked for a receipt for the tires and any other documentation to help identify the car. I then contacted his insurance company, asked for a copy of the claim, and called Detective Marks to update him on our progress.

He said, "You'll need a copy of the police report, which I'll email you. Having a local law enforcement contact would also be helpful. I'll make a call and include the contact information in the email."

"Thanks so much, Detective, I appreciate it."

"Good luck, Mr. Burnett."

With Mia in the city and nothing else to do the rest of the day, my mind drifted back to the nurse murders. Thinking about my next step, if I were still on the force, I called my former partner, Matt Frost, for his take on them.

"Detective Frost," he answered as if in a rush.

"Hey, Frosty."

His tone immediately cheerful, "Hi, Dan. It's been a while."

"Yeah, it has. How've you been?"

"I'm good, but these bodies floating up on the beach have the entire department on our toes."

"I can imagine. Do you have any inside information you can share?"

"I think it's all in the media. We're looking at a guy who attacked a nurse at Bellevue a couple of years ago, but I don't think there's anything there. Of course, we're looking at the victims for any link other than being a nurse."

"Jim and I are speculating on some theories, but nothing worth sharing yet."

"I'll bet you have," he laughed. "I can picture you guys sitting around the office, letting your imaginations run wild."

"I'm sure it's exactly as you imagine," I chuckled.

"How's Hannah doing?"

"Really well. She just took a job at Chase Bank as an executive assistant."

"Not bad for your first job out of school!"

"I'm proud of her. How's everything with your family?"

"Everyone's good."

"All right. Good talking to you, Frosty."

"You, too. Don't be a stranger."

BY THE END of the day, I had all the promised paperwork to take to the auction, received the call confirming the car was on site, and made a flight reservation to PBI the following morning.

While enjoying another fantastic dinner, Mia told me there would be a new Elsa Nordstrom special report on TV at 7:00, this one about Sierra Swan.

We tuned in just as the show began, and Elsa's narration over video images began with Sierra's first time on ice skates. We were told she was three years old at the time and saw her doing more walking than skating. Then, we saw her mother on camera telling us about Sierra's love for the outdoors. The family home was in Stamford, Connecticut, and we saw images of Sierra and her older sister paddling kayaks and canoes on a lake. There was a video of them sitting by a campfire with tents in the background during the girls' camping trips with their father, while both parents shared their memories of her.

After a commercial break, the next segment showed Sierra in her teenage years sailing dinghies and other small sailboats competing in races on Long Island Sound—a replay of my own childhood.

"Mia, those are the kind of boats I learned to sail on when I was a teenager."

"Looks like fun!" she said

With this half-hour program dedicated only to Sierra, Elsa went into more depth. There was a video of her at a yacht club holding trophies won while racing, and according to her mother, sailing was a primary focus of her teenage years.

The final segment was from the perspective of Sierra's fiancé. We saw him on the verge of tears, discussing their wedding plans. "We were all set to be married in June. The church and reception were booked, we had just received the invitations and were addressing the envelopes together. I'm going to miss her so much," he finally wept.

As Elsa wound up the story, we were again left wondering if there would be more young nurses killed. While these reports were well-produced human interest stories about the young women, they increased tension in the greater New York area. I knew the media aimed to keep this story in the public eye. Of course, they would claim to be merely responding to the public interest, but in reality, they were driven by the business of viewership and ratings.

Mia and I were deeply saddened by the story and sat in front of the TV for a few minutes, letting it sink in. Eventually, with a 7:00 am flight the next day, I went to bed early after packing a few necessities in a small overnight bag.

WHEN I ARRIVED in West Palm, it was still early. Stepping outside for a taxi, the heat and humidity of the tropical air washed over me. Florida always had a musty smell that I had never quite been able to identify. Perhaps it was the scent of flowers or freshly mown grass, or more likely, it was mold from the humidity.

After a short cab ride to the fairgrounds auction site, I asked for directions to the main office and was warmly greeted by Barry Johnson, a tall, distinguished gentleman with a pleasant smile. While we wandered out to the tent where the Aston was parked, he radioed for someone to meet us. I spotted the car right away in the middle of a row. The gleaming, light green metallic paint was unique to Aston Martin and appeared to be illuminated by a spotlight. Chris, the employee he had radioed, was waiting at the car, and the three of us reviewed all the paperwork I had with me.

Barry told me Chris was knowledgeable about Astons and knew where to look for numbers. He immediately noticed the non-riveted vehicle identification number behind the windshield. He then climbed under the back of the car and, using his phone as a flashlight, read out loud a number stamped on the differential. As he was reading, Barry and I confirmed that it matched the number on Michael Lerner's car and not the phony one under the windshield. Chris took a picture of the differential before climbing from under the vehicle and airdropped it to my cell phone.

"There's definitely something bogus about these numbers," Chris said.

"Well, we can't auction the car, so let's boot it," Barry instructed him, referring to a device placed on a tire to prevent the car from rolling.

"How do you recommend I get the car back?" I asked.

"You'll need to get the local sheriff's office involved. We'll abide by their order."

"Okay, I just so happen to have a contact there."

"Great. Get him out here, and when he's ready, let Chris or me know."

"Will, do. Thanks for your help." A sense of gratification washed over me.

"Anytime. It's better to have discovered this before the car was sold."

Two hours later, the Sheriff met me at the car, and I went through all the documents with him. When he saw me talking with the Sheriff, Chris came by and confirmed the car's numbers weren't correct. While we reviewed the paperwork with the Sheriff, Chris noted the tire receipt, which listed serial numbers. With that in hand, he kneeled at each tire and confirmed they matched the receipt supplied by my client.

When the Sheriff was convinced we had a legitimate claim to the car, he told me he would immediately impound it and follow up with the insurance company and Detective Marks in Connecticut. After reporting all this to a delighted Michael Lerner, I booked the next flight home.

While waiting for the flight at the airport, feeling proud and content, I called Jim to share my success. Within moments, he was planning a press release to further increase our popularity with the collector car community.

CHAPTER 8

On Friday morning, while eating breakfast, I received a call from Willy Grant, my police detective friend from Riverdale.

"Good morning, Dan."

"Hey, Willy, what's up?"

"I just got a call from Doug Morgan. He's the father of Natalie Morgan, the young woman you discovered on the beach."

"Yes. I saw him and his wife on TV."

"We spoke about the investigation, and he asked me for the name of a PI to hire to look into his daughter's death. I guess he's unhappy with the progress of the police so far."

"You mean the entire NYPD?" I quipped.

"That's correct. Before I gave him your name, I wanted to check with you first."

"I'd be willing to talk with him. I mean, the 'Nurse Murders' are already living in my brain, rent-free."

"I'm sorry to hear that," Willy chuckled.

"Give him my number. I'll let you know if anything comes of it."

"Okay, buddy. Good Luck!"

MIA WAS IN her library, and I stuck my head in the door and told her about Willy's call.

She said, "What's with you and all the high-profile cases?"

"It's just a phone call. I'm not sure what I can do that the entire NYPD can't do."

"Don't sell yourself short, love."

I just laughed as I turned and walked down the hall.

LATER THAT DAY, Doug Morgan called, sounding just as broken as when I saw him on TV. After introductions, I expressed my sorrow for his loss and asked how I could help.

"I'm hoping a fresh pair of eyes might have more success," he said.

"It's been three months since Natalie's abduction, and nearly a month since her body was discovered. The police have made no progress whatsoever."

"Perhaps, Mr. Morgan, but my partner and I don't have any-where near the resources NYPD does."

"Please, call me Doug, and I know that. But I also know from experience how bogged down in procedure government agencies can become. I'm thinking an independent approach might be worth a shot."

"Okay, to be honest, Doug, this case has already captured my interest. I'll look into it and let you know if I can help. We charge $85 an hour, plus expenses. How about if I send you a retainer agreement for $2000? That should roughly cover the first week, and I'll know by then if we can help."

"That will be fine, Mr. Burnett. Thank you."

"Okay, and please call me Dan. What's your email address?"

After he told me, I asked when he and his wife would be available to speak with me.

"Cindy and I are available anytime you are."

We agreed to meet at 10:00 at their home the following day and said our goodbyes.

Happy to be getting paid, I was eager to get started. After sending off the agreement, I spent the next few hours online, taking notes on everything reported in all three cases. This was my investigation method: I needed to be able to review what I knew and what I didn't know on a regular basis. Once I got further into it, there would be too much to keep track of in my head.

MIA EXITED HER library around 4:00 and announced she was done for the week. I made a shaker of martinis, and we sat in our happy place to unwind. She filled me in on her accomplishments, and I told her about my discussion with Natalie Morgan's father and our meeting the next day.

"You know, I was semi-serious earlier about you getting these high-profile cases," Mia said. "I can attest to your abilities, but how do you explain it?"

"I think it's either luck or just being in the right place at the right time."

Mia laughed before hugging my shoulder, "You're too modest, Dan."

THAT NIGHT, WE had a simple dinner of sliced grilled porterhouse, baked potatoes, and a salad from her garden. After eating, it had cooled enough to sit outside on the deck and enjoy the same view as from the living room. With a glass of cabernet in hand, we watched a colorful sunset over the Manhattan skyline. It was mostly orange between the cloud layers, with ribbons of magenta lower on the horizon, and we listened to small waves rolling in on the beach.

Doug and Cindy Morgan lived in one of the grand older homes on Netherland Avenue in Riverdale. I imagined how the neighborhood looked back in the Roaring Twenties, sitting high on a hill overlooking New York City, long before being surrounded by high-rises.

Both of them greeted me at the door, and, after introductions, they led me into the living room at the front of the house. It was tastefully furnished with overstuffed sofas and tall wing-back chairs in a classic style, with antique tables and heavy drapery. Cindy offered me coffee, but I declined.

The Morgans were about my age and dressed well. Cindy wore a black knee-length skirt and a white fitted blouse, while Doug wore dress slacks and a cardigan sweater. They appeared well-off and well-fed, so I had no worries about being paid. After expressing my sympathy, I asked them to tell me about Natalie.

Sitting side by side on a sofa holding hands, Doug began the conversation after taking a deep breath. "Natalie was an only child and grew up in this home. She was a homebody in high school, and while she was a good student, she didn't participate in sports or extracurricular activities."

With a tissue in hand, Cindy added, "Natalie always wanted to be a nurse, and enrolled in the nursing program at Hunter College as soon as she graduated high school."

When she handed me some pictures of their daughter, I saw the same happy face I had seen on television.

"Tell me more about her recent life," I said. "Did she belong to any groups? Was she involved with anyone romantically?"

"There were no organized groups, but she did get together with other nurses she went to Hunter with. Regarding romance, she dated a few times while in school, but nothing serious, which was surprising. I thought most girls that age have boys on the brain—I certainly did! We occasionally wondered if she was gay, but she never brought anyone around."

"Do you know the names of classmates she hung out with?"

"We know of one girl, Linda Stein, who was a friend of hers at school. Would you like us to contact her?"

"I can do that if you don't mind."

"We'll locate her contact info and email it to you," Doug said.

"How about the other missing young women? Did Natalie ever have any contact with either of them?"

"Not that we know of. When we learned there were others, we felt terrible for their families. We thought about calling them but were afraid we'd cause them more grief."

My initial impression of them was of an honest, professional couple who loved their daughter and were now heartbroken. I didn't pick up on anything odd from their body language, which was why I preferred meeting in person whenever possible. While I had no more questions, they seemed so eager to help, I tried to keep the conversation going, and said, "You've painted me a pretty good picture of Natalie; is there anything else I should know?"

It was then that Cindy's eyes welled up and she began to tremble, "How could anyone do this to these girls? I just don't understand!"

As sobbing consumed her, Doug tried to comfort her, and I felt compelled to respond. "I wish I could answer that, Mrs. Morgan, but I'm afraid I can't. There are cruelties in this world that no one can explain."

I had comforted parents many times over the years, and knew it was best to remain quiet and give Cindy time to compose herself. When she did, I said, "That's about all I have for today. Do you have any questions for me?"

They looked at each other for a moment, then shook their heads.

"Okay, thanks for making time for me today; I'll be in touch."

While driving back to Mamaroneck, I felt terrible for them. Over my career, I had met with the parents of missing or deceased children and was amazed at how they summoned the strength to go on. I thought about what I went through when Hannah was kidnapped, and realized that I'd also summoned the strength when it was needed most. Only now could I get a handle on it: you simply had no other choice.

MIA AND I spent the rest of the weekend on the boat, and Hannah joined us Sunday for a sail. It was just a typical easy weekend day sail—up the coast and back with a stop for lunch. Seeing the joy on Hannah's face while at the helm and watching her interact with Mia reminded me of how close I had come to losing her. The thought that Doug and Cindy would never see their daughter again haunted me all weekend.

The Morgans emailed Linda Stein's phone number over the weekend, and I tried calling her on Monday morning. When it went to voicemail, I sent a text instead. My message was short—just a request to contact me about Natalie. I then called Jim and told him what I was up to.

"Another high-profile case? What's up with that?"

"I can't explain it, Jim. Willy Grant was assigned the case, and the father asked him to recommend a PI, so he gave him my name."

"You're going to be the most famous PI in the country."

"That's only if I'm successful. And don't worry, I'll make sure you get some credit."

Laughing, he said, "Good luck with it, Dan. Let me know if I can help."

"You got it. I'll be in touch."

JUST BEFORE NOON, Linda Stein called. I identified myself as a detective working for the Morgans and thanked her for returning the call. I then expressed my sympathy for her friend's loss.

"We're all still in shock, Mr. Burnett. We can't believe she's gone; it's just horrible."

"When you say we, who are you referring to?"

"A few of us from the nursing school at Hunter College stay in touch. We get together for drinks on Friday nights with some other nurses."

"Did you always go to the same place?"

"Yes. The West Side Grill in White Plains."

"Did you know any of the other young women who went missing?"

"No. We didn't know them."

"Is there anything else that might help me with my investigation?"

After a pause, she said, "I can't think of anything."

"Would you text me the contact info for the other members of your Friday night group?"

"Sure. I can do that later today."

"Thanks so much, Linda. Again, I'm sorry for your loss."

After contemplating where to go next, I realized I'd have to involve the other victims' families. There was just no way around it.

I obtained their phone numbers, and my first call was to the parents of Sierra Swan—the most recent beach find. When Mrs. Swan answered the phone, I went through the same dialogue I had with my previous calls: identifying myself, who hired me, and expressing my sympathies. Then I asked, "Did I catch you at a bad time?"

"No, Mr. Burnett. How can I help you?"

"Did Sierra know any of the other missing nurses?"

"I don't think so. At least we never heard any of their names before."

"Did she belong to any groups or hang out with other nurses?"

"Not recently. She was engaged to be married and spent most of her time with her fiancé."

"Would you be kind enough to give me his name and number?"

"Sure, his name is Devan Wolfe." She paused momentarily to find his number and then read it to me.

"I'm just starting this investigation," I said, "and I'm trying to find any link between the young women. If you think of anything that might help, will you please let me know?"

"Certainly, Mr. Burnett. I'm happy to hear someone other than the police is looking into this."

"You can call me Dan. Thanks so much for your time, Mrs. Swan."

"It's Beth. Bye, Dan."

Before calling the other parents, I tried the fiancé. When he answered, I followed the same dialogue, ending with my sympathies.

"Thanks. How can I help you?"

"Did Sierra know any of the other nurses who went missing?"

"I never heard her mention any of those names."

"When was the last time you saw her?"

"That morning, when she went to work. We lived together."

"Do you believe she was abducted while leaving work?"

"I do. Her car was in the parking lot."

I sensed an impatience in his tone, which was a departure from how he answered the phone. But I pushed on. "Did she wear a uniform to work?"

"Yes. She left the house with it on and usually changed when she got home."

"I'm sorry to ask all these questions—I'm sure you've answered them all before, but I'm just starting my investigation."

"No problem, I'm happy to help."

"How well do you know her friends?"

"Pretty well. We had been going out for two years before we got engaged. I think I knew all her friends."

"Would you be kind enough to text me their names and numbers?"

"I'd be happy to. I'm glad to hear about your investigation. If you find the guy who did it, I'd love a crack at him before the cops get him."

"I can understand that, Devan. I look forward to receiving your list."

"I'll do it right now. Good luck with the investigation."

"Thanks."

While jotting notes after the call, I sensed he hadn't told me everything, but couldn't put my finger on why.

I'd been fortunate so far. People answered their phones and were willing to speak with me. Before cell phones, we would leave a message at their home while they were at work and hope they called back. We would always play phone tag and finally connect from home in the evenings. I've become a fan of technology.

THE NEXT MORNING, while gazing at the water, my mind went back to a previous thought I had about why the bodies were washing ashore in the same general area of Long Island Sound. The likely explanation was that that was where they were dumped. It could have been from the shore or a boat. Then I thought about the tides and currents in the Sound and the waters around New York City. I was sure the Hudson River drained out through the Verrazano Narrows into the Atlantic, but the Harlem and East Rivers met at Hell's Gate along northeastern Manhattan. As I'd experienced myself, the currents there could be severe.

I put those thoughts on the back burner and attempted to call the parents of Laura Kelly, the second body found. I knew Laura grew up in Dobbs Ferry, and from my research, I had the name, address, and phone number of the parents.

"Kelly residence, Peter speaking."

Surprised by the formal greeting, I said, "This is Dan Burnett. Doug Morgan hired me to investigate the death of his daughter."

"Yes, how are they doing?"

"About how you would imagine. I'm sorry about your loss."

"It's been a tough couple of months," his voice cracking.

"Am I catching you at a bad time?"

"No. I have all the time you need."

"Thank you, Peter. I'm just beginning my investigation and searching for anything linking the three young women."

"How can I help?"

"Is it possible that Laura knew either of the others?"

"We had never heard their names before all this."

"Where did she go to school?"

"SUNY, Westchester."

I went on to ask about groups, romantic relationships, where her car was found, and other things I had asked the others. Learning very little, I asked if he would text me a list of her friends with contact information.

"Sure. Shelly and I will do that this evening. Feel free to call anytime; I'm happy to help. This has been a pretty dark time for us, and this might be our opportunity to do something constructive. Or at least feel like it."

"I can assure you that you are, and I appreciate your time."

I WAS MENTALLY worn out from the phone calls with the families. There was a lot of emotion involved on their part, and I always felt like I was walking on eggshells. I spent another hour organizing my notes and setting up a spreadsheet to reconcile the friends' names as they came in. I planned to revisit it the following day.

I stuck my head in Mia's library and asked if she was ready for a cocktail.

"I thought you'd never ask!" she smiled.

WHILE PREPARING A shaker of Manhattans, Mia wandered into the kitchen and hugged me from behind, her touch comforting. After pouring them into martini glasses, we carefully carried them to our happy place, touched glasses, and said, "Cheers!"

"I heard some of your calls to the victim's parents. How did that go?" she asked.

"Okay. It's never pleasant making those calls and asking them to focus on their pain, but they received me well."

"You were very sensitive while speaking with them."

"Thank you. How was your week?"

"Great! We've completed the custom design, and the buyer is thrilled. We're sending it out for production next week."

"What would you like to do this weekend?"

"I have some more picking to do in the morning, and I'd like to start preserving the tomatoes."

"How about a boat day on Sunday?"

"Sounds good. See if Hannah would like to join us."

"Okay, I'll call her later."

As MIA WAS tending her garden, I sat down to reconcile the list of friends from everyone I'd spoken to. Fortunately, they had all sent an organized list of names, and most had contact information. When finished, one name appeared on two lists: Kayla Mateo. I tried calling, but when it went unanswered, I sent a text asking for a return call.

While organizing and reviewing my notes, I thought about how helpful it would be to contact each nurse's employer for a list of patients and reconcile those lists for common names. But understanding HIPAA laws, I knew that would never happen. I spent the rest of the morning transferring my notes and lists into a binder.

When Mia was done picking vegetables, she started jarring tomatoes—I estimated more than fifty. She boiled and peeled them, packed them in sterilized Mason jars, and cooked them again in their jars. A few hours later, she had nearly a dozen and said they would keep all winter. *Seems like a lot of work to me,* I thought to myself.

While she was doing that, I called Hannah.

"Hi, Dad."

"Hey, Han. Are you up for sailing tomorrow?"

"I'm glad you asked. Have you seen the weather forecast?"

"Not yet."

"Besides a nice sunny day, it'll be blowing fifteen to twenty out of the northeast!"

"Good to hear. Fall must be coming."

"I'd like to bring Ken if that's cool."

"Sure, I'd love to see him; It's been a while."

"Does 10:00 work?"

"Perfect. See you on the dock!"

I hadn't seen Ken since her graduation party, but I enjoyed having him on the boat. He's an accomplished sailor whose family kept a boat in Mystic, Connecticut.

While working on the tomatoes all afternoon, Mia had started a pot of Bolognese sauce for dinner that night. In addition to the usual ingredients, she cooked in finely diced carrots, celery, and onions— what she called mirepoix. Later that evening, she served it over spaghetti with garlic bread and a bottle of Montepulciano. *It was the best spaghetti I've ever had!*

CHAPTER 9

We had a vigorous sailing day with Hannah and Ken, and her weather forecast was spot-on. We flew across the sound, heeled over hard, wearing foul-weather jackets to protect us from the spray. I could see from the smiles on their faces that they were loving it. Mia, on the other hand, was uncomfortable with *Privateer* leaning over this much, but as she grew accustomed and saw how much we were all enjoying it, so did she.

When anchored in Hempstead Harbor, sheltered from the wind, we removed our jackets for lunch and enjoyed the beautiful day. We all knew we would run out of days like this soon enough.

Ken told us about his sailing adventures over the summer. He and his family took their boat to Maine, where they spent over a month exploring the bays and rivers along the rocky shoreline. He was animated and used his hands, reaching over his head, when he said, "The tide varied by nine to ten feet from high to low, and we had to climb ladders up to the docks. There was a harbor called Biddeford Pool that appeared normal at high tide but was just vast expanses of mud at low tide—the strangest transformation I'd ever seen!"

Having always wanted to sail to Maine, I found his account fascinating. After a downwind run back to City Island, Ken rinsed the salt off Privateer before he and Hannah left for the evening. While Mia and I were driving home, she asked about Hannah and Ken's relationship.

"I've wondered about that myself," I said. "She's been seeing him off and on for over a year, but they don't seem like lovers. I know they occasionally go out to eat and enjoy hiking and camping together. Maybe they've been intimate, but it doesn't seem serious to me."

"That's the impression I got as well. They seem more like friends than lovers," Mia added.

Monday morning brought cooler weather while the wind remained brisk. We could see the first signs of turning leaves on both sides of the Sound. After breakfast, while reviewing my case book, I noted that I'd not heard back from Kayla Mateo. I tried calling again, and this time, she answered. After my usual introduction as a PI working for the Morgan family, she apologized for not getting back to me.

"I'm sorry, Mr. Burnett. I was traveling this weekend, and it just slipped my mind. Please don't think I don't want to help. I worked with Natalie and went to school with Laura, so I'm freaked out!" she exclaimed.

"Did Natalie and Laura know each other?"

"I doubt it. I mean, like, we didn't hang out together or anything."

"You're also a nurse at Westchester Med, right?"

"Yes. We're all scared. I no longer wear my uniform outside the hospital. None of us do—we don't want anyone to know we're nurses."

"That's a good idea—keep it up. Has your employer posted guards in your parking lot?"

"Have they ever! We now have to show an ID when entering and exiting, and they patrol the lot looking for anything suspicious."

"Good to hear. I'm searching for some kind of connection. Is there anything you can think of that links the victims?"

"I know Natalie and some other nurses got together at a bar on Friday nights, but other than that, I see no connection."

"Do you know the other nurse's names?"

"I don't recall; I was only there once with Natalie. I would have remembered if they were the ones who were murdered, though."

"Okay, thanks for speaking with me. Feel free to call me if you think of anything that will help."

"I will, Mr. Burnett. And again, I apologize for not getting back to you right away."

"No problem. Bye now."

So, my one possible link didn't pan out. I considered where to go next and decided to try the family of Amy Patterson, the last of the missing nurses. After a quick internet search, I found the address and phone number in Elmsford.

"Hello."

"Is this Mrs. Patterson?"

"It is."

After my whole spiel, including my sympathies, I asked if there might be a good time to meet with me.

"Since my husband passed away and Amy has gone missing, I have nothing else to do. Would you like to come to my home?"

"That would be great. When is a good time for you?"

"How about 2:00 today? That will give me time to pick up around here."

"2:00 is fine, but please don't go to any trouble for me."

"It's no trouble, Mr. Burnett. Do you have the address?"

"I do. See you then."

Hearing that she was a widow was news to me, but I was happy to be meeting in person. Like with the Morgans, I'd get a much better feel for the situation.

AFTER A HALF-HOUR drive to Elmsford, my navigation app led me into a pre-World War II neighborhood. The homes were primarily bungalows and Craftsman-style, close together on quarter-acre lots. All the properties were well cared for, with neatly mowed lawns. I rang the bell after walking a few steps up to a full-length front porch.

When the door opened, I was greeted with a smile, "You must be Mr. Burnett. Come on in."

"Thank you, Mrs. Patterson. Please, call me Dan."

"Okay, Dan. I'm Joan."

Joan was a few years older than I and had styled hair—a natural mix of blonde and gray. Her dress had short sleeves, a matching belt, and accordion pleats on the lower half, a look I recalled from old movies from the sixties. I'm sure Mia could pin it down to the stars who wore them.

She led me into the living room near the front door. The furnishings appeared to have been updated, maybe eight to ten years ago, in what I thought was a Tuscan style in gold and deep red, with a Persian rug in similar tones. Joan gestured for me to sit, and on the coffee table was a silver tea service that she hovered over, pouring each of us a cup. I guessed she had been looking forward to sharing afternoon tea with someone.

"What a lovely home you have," I said.

"Thank you. I'm comfortable here."

After stirring a sugar cube into my tea, I asked, "Have you had any encouraging news about Amy?"

She let out a deep breath and said, "No. I held out hope for a while, but now I fear she's been killed like the other nurses."

"Is it possible that she ran off with a boyfriend?"

"No. I just saw Gary last week. He's as broken up as I am."

"Did she know any of the other missing nurses?"

"I don't think so. I've never heard those names before."

"Tell me about Amy. What did she like to do?"

"She was always outgoing and very popular. She went out just about every night with friends, partying somewhere. And since she started dating Gary, she was always with him."

"Did she belong to any clubs or have any hobbies?"

"Not really. I always tried to get her involved with our church, but she never showed an interest. I think most of her friends were other nurses."

"Would you be kind enough to send me a list of her friends?"

"I can do that. What's your email address?"

I gave it to her and asked, "Do you think Gary would do the same?"

"I'm sure he would. We've known him for years; he lives right around the corner. I'll ask and share your email address with him."

We chatted for a while longer while finishing our tea. Realizing I'd learned about all I could, yet pleased I could help her enjoy the afternoon, I rose and said, "Thank you, Joan. I appreciate you seeing me."

"Anytime, Dan. I hope you're successful—I'll pray for you."

LATER THAT EVENING, while helping Mia clean up after dinner, I got a phone call. From the caller ID, I saw it was Kayla Mateo.

"Mr. Burnett?" she asked

"Yes, Kayla. Did you think of something?"

"Listen, I'm really freaked out. Someone followed me home from work."

Sensing her stress, I asked, "What's your address?"

She gave me an address on Bedford Park Boulevard, a neighborhood in the Bronx I knew well.

"Is the person who followed you still there?"

"No. He drove away."

"I'm on my way. Don't open your door for anyone, and keep your phone handy."

"Thank you, Mr. Burnett."

Mia had stopped what she was doing and watched me intently, listening to my side of the conversation with concern.

"I'm going to run to the Bronx," I explained. "A nurse just had someone follow her home."

"Okay. Be careful, Dan," she said, her eyes looking into mine.

"I will, don't worry."

After ensuring my Glock was under the seat, I took I-95 toward Kayla's. While driving, I called Frosty.

"Hey, Dan. What's up?"

"A friend of the missing nurses just called me and said someone followed her home. I'm heading to her place now in Bedford Park."

"Do you want me to meet you there?"

"Let me make sure this isn't a wild goose chase. I just wanted to let you know because it's your beat."

"Okay, give me the address. If I don't hear from you in half an hour, I'm on my way."

I gave him the address with the apartment number and said, "Thanks, buddy."

Bedford Park was one of the nicer residential areas in the Bronx; Frosty lived not too far from there. When I arrived, I slipped the Glock into my jacket pocket and called Kayla so she'd know it was me when I rang the buzzer. She answered on the first ring. "Mr. Burnett?"

"Yes, I'm coming up."

"Okay, I'll buzz you in."

Once inside, I found her apartment on the third floor and knocked on the door. After seeing her shadow in the peephole, she opened the door and clung to me like a long-lost friend.

"Thank you for coming, Dan," Kayla said. She was a young Black woman in her early to mid-twenties, attractive and poised. She had long Fulani braids and big eyelashes, and when she moved her head, the ornaments in her braids made a clicking sound.

"It's okay," I told her. "Have you seen any signs of him again?"

"No. I've been watching the parking lot from my window."

"Good. Let me make a phone call, and then you can tell me about it."

After she gestured for me to sit on her sofa, I called Frosty and told him I was at the apartment and all was well. Kayla sat across from me and prepared to tell me the story while I took notes.

Kayla said, "After I left Westchester Med, I noticed a pickup truck following me. I didn't think much of it until after going through the drive-thru at McDonald's when I saw he was behind me again. He followed me here and stopped to watch me. It was creepy, and I was afraid to leave the car until he drove away."

"Can you describe the truck?"

"I don't know much about trucks, but it was black and medium-sized, not one of those monster trucks that're all jacked up with big tires."

"Did you see who was driving?"

"Some white guy. That's all I saw."

"How about a license plate?"

"I didn't get the numbers, but it was a New York plate. When I tried to read the numbers as he drove away, a trailer hitch blocked my view. But I could see the colors."

I wrote as fast as she spoke. "I'll share this information with Detective Frost at the 49th Precinct. I'm sure he'll follow up with you tomorrow."

"But now this guy knows where I live. I won't be able to sleep!"

"Is there anyone you can stay with tonight?"

"My brother and his family live in New Rochelle. I could go there."

"Good. Call him to confirm, and I'll follow you to make sure you get there."

"Really? You'd do that?"

"Sure. It's on my way."

Kayla called her brother, who told her to come, and I followed her Honda Civic to his house. When I saw him greet her at the door, I waved and continued toward Mamaroneck. On the way, I called Frosty with the details, and he said he'd reach out to Kayla in the morning.

Although it was late, Mia had waited up for me, reclined in our happy place, reading a book. She was anxious to hear about my evening and relieved I'd returned safe and sound. After sharing the details and winding down a bit, we called it a day.

CHAPTER 10

Frosty called while I was eating breakfast. I swallowed the last strawberry and answered.

"Good morning, Dan. I just spoke to Kayla."

"How did she sound?"

"Still scared, but she's going to work."

"Was she able to remember anything more about the truck?"

"No, but it sounds like a Japanese make the way she described it."

"Did she give you anything else to go on?"

"Nothing. Without a plate number, a BOLO will be useless."

"True that. Is there any point in staking out the Westchester Med parking lot?"

"That would be up to the Valhalla police department. I'll give them a call."

"Okay. Keep me posted."

While adding notes to the case book, Frosty texted me that the Valhalla Police would share the pickup truck information with the security guards. That was about all we could ask for. I called Kayla and asked how she was doing.

"I'm okay, but I'll stay at my brother's until this whole thing is over."

"That's understandable. Will you be leaving work before dark?"

"I'm out at four today; why do you ask?"

"I'd feel better knowing you won't be driving alone after dark."

"Thanks for your concern, Dan. I'm sure I'll be fine."

"Try to keep yourself among other people, and if you see anything odd, call me or Detective Frost."

"Okay, I will."

LATER THAT AFTERNOON, I drove to Valhalla and parked along the street a half-mile south of Westchester Medical Center, hoping to spot the pickup if he followed her again. A little after four, I saw Kayla drive by in her Honda. Four vehicles behind her was a black Chevy pickup. I followed.

One car was between us, but I could see the truck had New York plates and a trailer hitch, as Kayla had described. While it wasn't jacked up, it was a full-size truck, not a mid-size. But then again, she said she didn't know much about trucks. We headed south on the Sprain Brook Parkway toward Kayla's brother's house in New Rochelle.

When she got off the ramp to the Cross County Parkway, the pickup did the same, and I followed. She got off at the Eastchester Road exit with us behind her. Knowing where her brother lived, I was sure that was where she was heading, and I assumed she wasn't aware of either of us behind her. The black pickup continued toward the town center when she entered her brother's neighborhood. Following the truck, I scribbled the plate number on my pad.

When the pickup parked in front of a sports bar, I passed and pulled in a few spots ahead of him. I watched the driver in my mirror, a white guy, as he walked inside. I waited a few minutes before following him in.

I found him sitting at a table with a few other guys. He was around thirty, average in every way except for full sleeves of tattoos. One of the other guys at the table was wearing hospital scrubs. I sat at the bar just a few feet beyond them and ordered a Heineken. There were TVs on every wall just a few feet apart, and each showed a different game or sports talk show with the sound off and subtitles scrolling. Between the TVs were team jerseys and other memorabilia.

Sitting close enough to hear the discussion at the table behind me, it sounded like they were all nurses. I had initially thought the guy in the scrubs might be a doctor, but after eavesdropping, they were all ragging on doctors. They joked about what a mess one doctor had made of someone's hip replacement and were making bets on when the patient would be back for repair.

After finishing my beer, I headed for Mia's and called Frosty on the way.

"Hi, Dan. What's up?"

"Hey, are you at the station?"

"Yup. For another few minutes."

"Can you run a plate for me?"

"Sure."

"New York tag TGY-142. A Black Chevy pickup."

"I'll call you right back."

While driving, I thought this guy in the black pickup was worth looking into. Believing he'd followed Kayla home, he sounded like some kind of stalker, and if he was a nurse himself, maybe he had a connection to the murdered young women. I felt like I was onto something.

As I pulled into Mia's driveway, Frosty called. "The plate belongs to James Dennis, 1 Clinton Park, New Rochelle. I think that's one of the high-rise apartments near New Roc City. I ran him through the system and found only some old traffic violations."

"Thanks, buddy. I appreciate it."

"Take care, Dan."

AFTER ANOTHER WONDERFUL meal with Mia, I retrieved the case book and made entries for everything that had happened over the last two days. Mostly, it was my discussion with Amy Patterson's mother, the encounter with Kayla Mateo, and the black pickup. Once it was all in the book and I knew where to find it, my mind was clear to focus on James Dennis. Since I had spotted him just south of Westchester Med, I assumed he worked there, and I planned to confirm that by following him to work.

THE NEXT DAY, I woke early to be in New Rochelle before James Dennis left for work. When I arrived at his address, I saw that Frosty was correct. It was the Clinton Park Apartments, and there was a parking garage. I entered and found his truck on the third level. Seeing no one around at this early hour, I took a magnetic tracking device from my glove compartment and placed it under his right front wheel well. After confirming it was linked to my phone, I exited the garage, parked nearby, and sipped coffee while waiting for him to drive out.

Shortly after 8:00, he did. Remaining a few cars back, I followed James on the reverse route we drove yesterday, back to Westchester Medical Center, where I took a few pictures as he entered the employees' parking lot. Now that I knew he worked there, I wondered how to follow up and thought of texting Kayla and asking for a callback. Not wanting to identify my suspect, I followed a common practice at the department to avoid leading a witness. I would ask her about three names. It was only minutes later when she called.

"I got your text," she said.

"Yes, thanks for the callback. Have you had any more followers?'

"No. Thanks for checking on me."

"Based on our investigation, we're curious about three people. Let me bounce some names off you: Ted Smith, James Dennis, and Donna Rooney. Are any of those names familiar?"

"The only one I know is Jim Dennis, or James, as you said. He's a nurse here, and a real creep. He's covered in tattoos and always watches me when I walk by; it feels like he's undressing me with his eyes."

Trying not to dwell on him, I said, "So the other names are unfamiliar?"

"I've never heard of them. Do they work at Westchester Med?"

"I don't know; they're just names we're following up on."

"Do you want me to check the employee directory?"

"Not necessary. What department does Jim Dennis work in?"

"Post-op, I think. I usually see him there wheeling patients in and out."

"Okay, that's all I have today, Kayla. How are things working out at your brother's?"

"Fine. I'm having a lot of fun with my nieces."

"Good to hear. Sorry to bother you."

"Anytime, Dan."

I had enough information on James Dennis to consider him a suspect. He worked in the same place as Natalie, and he could be stalking Kayla. I called Willy to get his take on it.

"Did you have any luck with the Morgans?" he asked.

"Yeah, thanks for the referral. They hired me, but I'm not sure I can help them. Are you still on the case?"

"Every day. Bella, too. For some reason, the department made us the lead detectives. I guess because we were the first ones to work it."

"Maybe it's because you're good detectives."

Laughing, he said, "We'll see how good we are. With the missing women residing in multiple counties, I spend most of my time coordinating between the local departments and the State Police."

"Let me bounce something off you."

"Shoot."

"A nurse at Westchester Med had a guy in a pickup follow her home. I found out his name, and it turns out he's also a nurse at Westchester Med, where Natalie Morgan worked."

"Interesting. Send me his information; Bella and I will see if we can link him to anything else."

"Thanks, Willy. You'll have it in a minute."

"Good. I'll let you know what we find out."

After ending the call, I debated hanging around in Valhalla to follow Jim Dennis home again, but with the tracking device, I could locate him anytime. I returned to Mamaroneck.

Later that afternoon, I opened the tracking app and saw him driving south into New Ro. A few minutes later, he stopped at the same sports bar as the day before.

CHAPTER 11

While sipping coffee, I added more notes to the casebook. Once up to date, I leafed through it and saw my notes of curiosity about the currents around New York City and western Long Island Sound. From my years on the water, I knew how the tides came and went, and I imagined something floating on or just below the surface would move with them. But maybe there was a deeper current I wasn't aware of. I thought of whom I could ask and figured the National Oceanic and Atmospheric Administration would be the best place to start.

I searched online for their closest office and found the Eastern Region Headquarters in Bohemia, New York. Using Google Maps, I saw it was on Long Island, near Islip Airport, about an hour and a half's drive away. After eating breakfast with Mia, I gathered my notes, told her where I was going, and headed for Long Island.

Upon arrival at the NOAA facility, I went through security, which included walking through a magnetometer similar to those used at airports. I assumed this was now standard procedure at government buildings. I noticed thick concrete barriers outside the front door to prevent a vehicle loaded with explosives from crashing through.

At the front desk, I asked to speak to someone about tides and currents around New York City. A few minutes later, I was greeted by Todd McDougall, a young man I guessed to be in his late twenties. After introducing myself and explaining why I was there, he brought me back to his cubicle and offered me a chair.

"So, you're investigating the murdered nurses that washed up in the Sound. How can I help?" he asked.

"As a long-time sailor of these waters, I understand the tides. But I wonder if other overriding currents would explain these bodies washing up in the same area."

"Let's take a look." Todd made a few keystrokes on his computer, which brought up a screen showing New York Harbor and western Long Island Sound. From a dropdown menu, he brought up an animation of real-time currents. He set that image to show the last six hours and the forecasted next six hours, and let it run. We watched the water flow east to west and back to the east as the tide rose and fell.

"What if a body were dropped in one of the rivers along the east side of Manhattan?" I asked.

With a few more keystrokes, Todd zoomed in on the area around Hell's Gate and set the animation in motion for historical currents. We watched as the flow from the Harlem River joined the East River in a turbulent manner, with some of the flow heading into the sound and some into the East River on an ebb tide. When the flood tide started, it reversed course. Todd then said, "I think that any floating object would just go back and forth with the changing tide and not progress in one direction over time."

"Are there any spots in the area that would flow over time toward Mamaroneck or Sands Point?" I asked.

"Let's see."

He zoomed back out and put that area in motion. We watched for a few minutes, and he tracked the speed of the flooding and ebbing tides. Over a week-long sample, he found that the speeds matched, suggesting that any object would just drift back and forth. I then asked if that would change with the seasons.

"No. We've never recorded a seasonal change," he explained. "The only thing I could imagine would be during a hurricane that lingered in the area, where the wind would affect the flow over a few days. Let's see what happened during Hurricane Sandy."

With more keystrokes, he returned to October 29th, 2012, and let the animation run. Over the following two days, we saw the water flooding in at double the average speed and barely flowing out during the ebb.

Todd said, "So, here's a case where if something was floating in the water east of Sands Point, it could wash up there."

"But that was twelve years ago, and we've had no similar events since."

"Correct. In the case of these bodies you're referring to, my guess is they were dumped from a boat in the vicinity. The wind could have blown them a few miles north or south toward the coasts of the Sound," Todd concluded.

I contemplated what else I should ask while Todd eagerly awaited another question. When I came up with none, I said, "Thank you for your time, Todd. You've been a big help."

We exchanged cards as he walked me out.

So far, none of my efforts have panned out. I had found no links between the young women other than that they were nurses who wore uniforms, and a few of them had drinks on Friday nights. My theories on tides and currents had been disproven, and I was back to square one. While driving, I realized the only suspect I had was James Dennis, and if that led nowhere, I might have to tell Doug and Cindy Morgan that I couldn't help them.

When I returned to Mia's, it was late afternoon, and after fighting the traffic, it felt like cocktail hour to me. But I found her in the kitchen drinking cranberry juice. Assuming this was one of her healthy days, I grabbed a Heineken from the fridge, disappointed to be drinking alone. She told me we were having Bolognese again tonight, and she would freeze anything left over.

While she was preparing dinner, I sat down with my laptop and went through two days' worth of emails. I was pleased that Joan Patterson and Amy's boyfriend Gary Leonard had sent me their lists. After adding the names to the spreadsheet, I felt better about my prospects.

Mia announced dinner was ready, and we sat down to her Bolognese, which hadn't lost anything in reheating. I then understood why she went to the effort of preserving the homegrown tomatoes. She served it with zucchini from her garden, sautéed in olive oil and garlic.

When I asked about her day, Mia said, "The woman we did the custom design for last week loved it so much that we're doing one for her friend. I spoke with her today, and I've already started sketching."

"That's fantastic. It sounds like your business is taking off."

"I hope so. I'm enjoying it and making money, too!"

"Good for you, sweetheart."

"Would you care to celebrate by joining me for a bath after dinner?"

I leaned across the table and kissed her. "You must have read my mind."

The next morning, Mia and I had our usual breakfast of berries and yogurt while watching the news. They were still focused on the murdered nurses, but there was nothing new to report.

Mia went upstairs to dress, and I returned to my dining room workstation and checked the tracking app on my phone; James' pickup was still in the parking garage. I opened my laptop, reviewed where I'd left off, and focused on my latest spreadsheet entries from Joan Patterson and Gary Leonard. I ran another reconciliation with the new additions. A new common name popped up: Rebecca Yates, another nurse from Westchester Medical. She was friends with Amy, Natalie, and their common friend, Linda Stein. Rebecca's name came from Amy's mother, but she was not on the list from Gary Leonard. Neither was Natalie Morgan, and I wondered why. Since I already had a text thread going with Linda, I texted her about Rebecca.

Ten minutes later, she called. "How's the investigation going, Mr. Burnett?"

"Please, call me Dan, and thanks for the callback. I'm still gathering information and have found a common name among people I've spoken to. Rebecca Yates was on your list, and it's also on a list from Amy Patterson's mother.

"Yes. Amy and Rebecca are part of our Friday night group, but they didn't go to Hunter. Natalie knew Rebecca from Westchester Medical. In fact, I saw her last week."

"Might you share her phone number with me?"

"Sure. I'll text you her contact info."

"Do you, by chance, know Kayla Mateo?"

I had asked about Kayla just to keep track of who knew who.

"Maybe. I think she also worked at Westchester Medical. She may have attended one of the Friday night things, but she wasn't a regular."

"Okay. Thanks, Linda."

"Anytime, Dan."

A moment later, I received Linda's text with Rebecca's contact info, and I made the call. She answered on the first ring, and after going through my now well-rehearsed introduction, I asked if she knew of any other connections between the missing nurses—clubs, classes, groups, or whatever. It sounded like she was driving.

"I don't," Rebecca said. "All the nurses I know are trying to piece together anything common. There just isn't anything other than leaving work in a uniform."

"You work at Westchester Med, correct?"

"That's right."

"Do you know Kayla Mateo?"

"I don't think so. It's a big place."

"What can you tell me about the Friday night bar get-togethers?"

"There's not much to tell. We're just a few nurses who had a drink together on our way home for the weekend. We haven't met since Amy disappeared."

"Can you tell me the names of the other nurses?"

"The regulars were Linda Stein, Natalie Morgan, Amy Paterson, and me. Occasionally, someone might bring another friend, but we were the 'core four,' as we like to call ourselves."

"Thank you for speaking with me, Rebecca."

"No problem. I hope you find that motherfucker!"

After ending the call, I burst out laughing. While I'd heard that term many times before and used it occasionally, I was surprised to hear it from a woman.

After rechecking the tracking app, I saw James was northbound on the Sprain Brook Parkway, no doubt on his way to work. Now that I had the tracking information, I thought I'd record his location to see where he went. However, I was still concerned about him following Kayla.

I WAS RUNNING out of things to investigate. If I were still with the NYPD, we would turn to forensics at this point in the investigation. They would have done fiber analysis on the blanket and rug used to wrap the bodies, as well as the rope. While I was sure they had, I knew better than to ask Willy to share that info with me. There would be hell to pay if it were to become public knowledge. But after some thought, I saw no reason not to share what I had learned with him.

"Good morning, Willy. Anything new?"

"Not much. How about you?"

"Well, I can tell you that after searching for any link between the murdered women, I've found nothing other than they're nurses," I admitted.

"Same here. The bodies were so decayed that forensics had nothing to work with. We have no idea if they were sexually assaulted, poisoned, or whatever. One had been partially eaten by marine life—Sierra Swan."

"I looked into tides and currents to see if I could narrow down where the bodies were dumped, but came up with nothing. I'm going with the premise they were dumped off a boat."

"Why's that?"

"I went to the NOAA office on Long Island and sat with an expert on tides and currents. We couldn't replicate any conditions under which the bodies would end up where they did."

"You are one dogged detective, Dan. Thanks for sharing that with me."

If there were ever an opening for Willy to share information, this would be the time. He said softly, "Keep this under your hat, but forensics determined two of the young women had broken neck vertebrae. They don't know if that was the cause of death, or if they were broken later—maybe while being disposed of."

"Interesting," I replied, knowing not to push it further.

"Well, good luck with it, Dan. I need to run."

"Okay, Willy. Be good."

While digesting this new bit of information, I wondered how likely it would be for their necks to break when they were thrown overboard. I imagined myself tossing a body off the side of a boat. I concluded that if their head struck the rail, it might break their neck; otherwise, it was unlikely.

Disappointed that I had no breakthroughs and used up all the time covered by the Morgan's retainer, I thought I should let them know I'd struck out. I wrote an account of my time, summarized what I had learned, and emailed it to them, requesting a call back if they had any questions. Twenty minutes later, Doug Morgan called.

"Hello, Dan. I got your email."

"Good. I don't want to take any more of your money if I'm not progressing."

"I appreciate your honesty. Let's leave it there, but we can renew our agreement if you come upon something new to investigate."

"Perfect. I'll be following the story anyway."

Later that afternoon, I checked the tracking app and saw that James was still at Westchester Med. So far, it seemed he just went to work and stopped at the bar on the way home—wash, rinse, and repeat. I had hoped by now that I would have seen him drive to the waterfront, either to go out on a boat or dump a body,

With nothing more to do, I watched TV while waiting for Mia to come home. The news was still all about the nurse murders and the latest disappearance. The media had set up reporters at multiple hospital employee parking lots and spoke with nurses as they were leaving. One of them explained, "We've all taken the advice not to wear uniforms in public, but we're still afraid."

When I heard the garage door open, I shut off the TV. As Mia entered the house, I greeted her with a hug and asked about her day.

"Just another day sketching dresses, but Sandy and I seem to be on the same page and getting along well," she said, sounding tired.

After setting down her things, she asked, "How about making us a cocktail, love? I'm beginning to understand why all commuters have a cocktail after making it home."

"Two Manhattans coming right up!"

When we were seated in the living room with our drinks, we touched our glasses and took our first sips. "Tell me about your day," Mia said.

"I ended my contract with the Morgans today. There's nothing more I can do for now."

"How did they take it?"

"Fine. He thanked me for my efforts and offered to reengage if something new came up."

"That sounds fair."

"I just didn't want to run up the bill with nothing to show for it."

She nodded, took another sip, and said, "So, now that you're no longer being paid to investigate this case, are you going to leave it alone?"

After a few moments, I replied, "We'll see."

"Uh huh," she smiled knowingly.

MIA MADE ANOTHER excellent dinner that evening: seared scallops over a bed of mixed greens with a lemon and dill vinaigrette. Other than the Bolognese, we seem to go months without repeating a meal.

As I lay in bed that night, I recalled my discussions with Willy, specifically about telling him I'd concluded the bodies were dumped from a boat. I tried to imagine how someone could carry a body down the docks without being seen.

A human body is a bitch to carry—a hundred-plus pounds of dead weight with no good way to grip it, and holding all that in your arms would ruin your back within a minute. Carrying it over your shoulder would be better, but it would undoubtedly attract attention. Perhaps you could make it down a dock at night without being observed, but it would be risky with cameras everywhere these days.

I then realized I was picturing a boat big enough to be kept at a dock, but what about a small, trailerable runabout? I'd seen them launched at boat ramps thousands of times, and someone could load a body in the privacy of their garage. Eventually, I fell asleep with that image in my mind.

AFTER MY FIRST cup of coffee, I googled boat launch ramps near me. More than a dozen were between the Connecticut state line and the western end of the Sound, all the way around to Northport, Long Island. After a quick breakfast, I headed to City Island to eyeball the launch ramp there. Once at the ramp, I watched people launch their boats from trailers pulled mainly by pickups. Of course, every truck had a trailer hitch, just like the one on James Dennis's pickup.

Once the boats were afloat, they would tie them to a dock, park their trucks and trailers, then return to cast off into the Sound. I was surprised by how many trailers were in the parking lot already that morning, but then again, fishermen were often out before sunrise. I watched a few more launches and realized no one would notice a body if it were stashed on the floor in any of these boats.

Having seen all I needed to, I drove a few blocks over, parked at my marina, and wandered down to *Privateer*. I made coffee to ward off the morning chill and thought more about the missing nurses. Even though I was no longer being paid, the case was under my skin, and I couldn't let it go. I called Willy to share my new theory.

"Good morning, Willy. Here's my latest thinking."

Laughing, he said, "Let's hear it."

"Assuming the bodies are being dumped from a boat, I think it would be unlikely for someone to walk down a dock with a body, load it into a boat, and not be seen. But what if it was a trailered boat, and they loaded the body in their garage, then launched the boat, and dumped it in the Sound with no one around?"

After a moment, he said, "That makes a lot of sense, but what are we supposed to do, surveil all the launching ramps? There's a shit load of 'em."

"There are fifteen in the vicinity, and you'd need drones to look into the boats. You couldn't see a body looking at the side of a boat from a ramp."

"I see you've given this a lot of thought."

"You know me."

"That I do!" he laughed.

"Here's another kicker: James Dennis's pickup has a trailer hitch."

"Did you give me info on him already?"

"Yes, just a couple of days ago."

"I remember. We haven't gotten to him yet."

"I know how it is."

"Let me bounce this off of Bella. Maybe she'll have some ideas on how to round up the resources to watch the boat ramps."

"All right, Willy. Thanks for hearing me out."

"Anytime, pal."

CHAPTER 12

On my way back to Mamaroneck, I drove along the coast instead of the highway, hoping to find more launching ramps. After passing through New Rochelle Harbor, a few police cars passed by with lights and sirens—the whole show. Wondering if this could have something to do with discovering another body, I followed them to the beach at Hudson Park. After parking, the cops rushed to the beach on foot, where a gathering had already formed. I followed a ways back, and as I got closer, the smell hit me: decaying human flesh.

I watched the seagulls inspect a rolled-up blanket lying in the surf, wrapped with rope, similar to the one I had seen before. I backtracked a bit to find a seat and escape the smell. It wasn't long before Elsa Nordstrom showed up, followed by a camera crew in a van with a satellite dish. Within a minute, she was broadcasting live from the beach, framing the shot with the body and the police directly behind her. I was amazed at how quickly the media could respond.

A half-hour later, the coroner arrived with a crew wearing HAZMAT suits, loaded the body in their van, and drove off. They were on the scene for less than five minutes.

As everyone dispersed, Elsa walked past me, and I said, "Excuse me. Have you been to all of these beach finds?"

She paused to look at me and said, "Beach finds? That's an interesting way to put it."

"I'm sorry, I suppose that sounds insensitive. I've seen you on TV whenever one of these young women washed ashore."

She stepped closer, extended her hand, and said, "I'm Elsa Nordstrom. Who might you be?"

I noticed a Swedish accent that did not come across on TV. Besides the blonde hair, she had striking blue eyes and a chiseled face with sharp, high cheekbones.

"I'm Dan Burnett, a private investigator."

Looking at me curiously, she asked, "And what do you investigate?"

I wondered if she thought I was coming on to her. "Right now, I'm investigating the nurse murders."

She raised her eyebrows, also blonde. "Maybe we should compare notes."

"I agree, maybe we should."

I still sensed she thought I was coming on to her when Elsa said, "Give me your contact information; I'll call you later."

We exchanged business cards before I watched her drive off in a white Porsche Boxster with a navy blue top, following the satellite van. I knew she would research my name before contacting me.

I WALKED IN the door to find Mia in front of the TV, watching a replay of the scene I'd just witnessed. After a quick kiss, I told her I was on the beach when the police arrived. Seeing the surprise in her eyes, I explained I'd been driving along the coast and followed cops to the scene.

"So you just happened to be in the area?"

"Yup. Are you ready for a cocktail?"

"Sure. How about a Cosmopolitan today?"

"Sounds good," I replied, going to the bar cabinet. When I finished with the shaker, I poured the pink elixir into Martini glasses, then handed her one and sat beside her, watching the news loop.

"I spoke with this reporter today on the beach."

"Elsa? Is that her name?"

"Yes. We exchanged cards so we could compare notes."

"She's really quite beautiful."

"Yeah, she has a Swedish accent when speaking in person."

Mia pursed her lips and said nothing more. Sensing a note of jealousy in her reaction, I remained quiet. I thought of changing the subject, but after a moment, I wondered how long it would take to identify the body. I guessed that would take another day, and I also thought it would be Amy Patterson.

THE FOLLOWING DAY, we learned that it was, indeed, Amy. I sat by the TV, feeling terrible for Joan Patterson while sipping coffee. Mia joined me a few minutes later and asked, "Is that who you thought it would be?"

"Yes. Amy Patterson. Her mother prayed for me to find her."

WITH THIS LATEST discovery, New York was in a frenzy. Each television network had its usual panel of reporters blaming the police for not solving the case and not having even one suspect after all this time. The Post and Daily News had front pages with three-inch headlines over a full-page photo of the tied-up bundle rolling in the surf. I recalled how, as a cop, media frenzies always turned up the pressure, and I knew the police would double the number of officers assigned to the case, if only to appease the public. If something didn't break soon, the public would become hostile.

A minute later, my intuition proved correct. The network advised us to stay tuned for a police department press conference to be held shortly. Mia rose to cut a fresh pineapple into spears for breakfast. By the time we had finished eating a few pieces, the press conference started.

A podium was set up in front of One Police Plaza. With the press gathered around and protesters holding signs demanding justice for the nurses, the Chief of Police addressed the crowd.

"Good morning, everyone. I wanted to bring you up to date on our efforts regarding the murdered young women. We do believe these are serial-style incidents and are investigating accordingly. While we don't yet have a definitive suspect, we are closing in on the motivation behind the killings."

He paused a moment for a sip of water, scanned the crowd, and then continued. "We are coordinating with the neighboring towns and have assigned more personnel to the case to pursue all the leads coming in. I can assure you this is our number one priority, and with the assistance of the surrounding police departments, we anticipate an arrest soon. I have time for a few questions."

The press erupted, everyone shouting to be heard. When the Chief pointed to someone for his question, the others quieted to let him speak.

"Are all these cases linked because they're nurses?"

"At this time, it appears to be that way," he responded.

"Should all nurses be afraid?" asked another reporter.

"I understand most nurses no longer wear uniforms outside of their work. That is good advice, and they should continue doing so."

Elsa asked the next question: "Why are all the bodies being found in the same general area when they live and work in various places?"

"We don't have an answer for that yet, but we're working on it."

Mia and I watched as reporters reworded each other's questions, and the Chief did the same with his answers. When the Chief finally stepped off the podium, Mia exclaimed, "He told us nothing!"

"That's because he has nothing. That was just an effort to appease the public and show they're working—an attempt to turn down the heat."

"That was weak," she said in disgust.

I reached for her hand. "You're right."

LATER THAT MORNING, while Mia was working in her library, I checked the tracking app to see if James's pickup had been anywhere near a launching ramp. Seeing that it had not, I again reviewed the case book to confirm what I knew and what I didn't know.

After reviewing the common friend spreadsheet again, I reflected on my discussions with the families and felt discouraged. I'd felt this way a few other times while at the department. I learned then that I couldn't let myself get too close to the emotions and stay dispassionate and objective. Staying dispassionate would be the hard part for me.

I thought a psychological profile of the killer might give me some direction, so I called my psychologist friend, Anne Gibbs. I'd met her while recovering from a gunshot wound a few years back, and she recently helped me with another case. She also gave me the referral for Hannah.

"This is Anne," she answered.

"Hi, Doc. Dan Burnett calling."

"Hey, Dan. How's your daughter doing?"

"Great. She just got a job with Chase Bank."

"Good to hear. What can I do for you?"

"I'm sure you're following the Nurse Murders?"

"Of course. How could I not?"

"Can you do an off-the-cuff profile of the perp?"

"Don't tell me you have another high-profile, national interest case."

"Well, it's off the record for the moment."

"Wow. Where should I start?"

"I don't know. I'm just trying to understand the motivation here."

After a moment, she responded, "Okay. I assume it's a he, and the crimes somewhat fit the M.O. of the Gilgo Beach murders or the Son of Sam. Given that these are all young females, there's likely a sexual element at play. I would assume that after capturing them, he's raping or abusing them somehow before killing them. Given the time between when they went missing and when they were found, he may be holding them captive and abusing them repeatedly before discarding them."

"What profile should I be looking for?"

"It could be anyone of active sexual age. That means from sixteen to sixty, and they must be strong enough to overcome the victims. It could even be a couple looking to play out a sexual fantasy."

"Okay, I assumed the first part, but the latter is a curveball."

"It's just a possibility, but one that needs to be considered."

"Tell me your thinking."

"In this modern age of multi-sexuality and pornography, more people are into kinks that would have been considered depravity a few years ago. The demographic of porn watchers increasingly includes young women, so what is considered 'normal' behavior is changing."

"I'm with you so far."

"Additionally, people can connect with others with similar interests on social media and dating sites."

"I appreciate your insight on this—you've opened a whole new avenue to consider."

"Anything else?"

"No. Thanks, Anne."

"Not a problem. Good luck!"

I SAT FOR a while to digest what Anne had told me, trying to open my imagination to these new possibilities. I reviewed everything in the book with a fresh perspective, focusing on the facts I was familiar with. But after an hour, the facts simply remained that a nurse's life had ended at the hands of someone else. It didn't matter if the killer was male or female or a couple. They all washed up between one and two months after being reported missing. What I didn't know was how long they were in the water before washing ashore. From the level of decay, I assumed it had been quite a while, but I needed a more accurate estimate.

I called Willy, hoping to trade some information.

"How you doin', man?"

"All good, but I'm no longer working for the Morgans. After a week, I didn't feel they were getting their money's worth."

"You're an honest man."

"Yeah, but I'm still interested in the case. I'm hoping we can share some information."

"What do you have to share?"

I told him about my spreadsheet of common friends and Anne Gibbs's potential profile of the perp.

"Her perp profile pretty much matches ours. But we don't have as comprehensive a list of common friends as you do."

"I'll forward you the spreadsheet."

"Thanks. What can I help you with?"

"I'd like to know how long the bodies were in the water."

"Forensics says between two and four weeks."

"So, if we follow Anne Gibbs's profile, the perp, or perps, could have kept the victims for a while before dumping them."

"For sure."

"Good to know. Thanks, Willy."

After contemplating the entire scenario, I assumed he, or they, hooked up with the young women and had their way with them for at least a few days. There would be no reason just to snatch them, kill them, and dump them in the water. I began to think the original theory of some guy with a nurse fetish was the most likely. Or possibly a couple with a nurse fetish.

MIA CAME OUT of her library to make lunch. She made us salads and explained that she needed to lose a few pounds to fit into a dress she wanted to wear.

I can't imagine where the weight will come from, I thought to myself.

After lunch, looking to change my focus, I drove to the marina to prepare *Privateer* for hauling. She was scheduled to be hauled at the end of the week, and now that we were done sailing for the season, there were a host of things to be done. My dock mate, Vinny, was also there prepping his boat. With barely a breath of wind, we took advantage of the opportunity and helped each other remove and bag our sails, which was a significant accomplishment—the only task that required two people to complete. I could pick away at the rest myself over the rest of the week.

I RETURNED TO the marina the following morning to tackle the final chores. Around midday, Willy called with some information on James Dennis.

"I don't think he's our guy, Dan."

My shoulders sagged as I let out a breath. "What did you find out?"

"According to DMV, there is no record of James Dennis ever registering a trailer of any kind, and his truck was registered on August 25th of this year, just one day before his employment began at Westchester Medical Center."

"It sounds like he just moved here."

"That would be correct. Before that, he was under the Atlantic Ocean on a nuclear submarine. He completed his enlistment as a hospital corpsman with the Navy on August 20th, long after three of the nurses went missing."

"Shit! There goes that suspect," I sighed, feeling defeated.

"No worries, buddy. It happens."

"I feel foolish."

"Don't. You had no way to do the research without police credentials, and I apologize for not following up on him sooner."

"It's not on you, Willy."

"Would you like some good news?"

"I could use some."

"Since there's no way we'll have the personnel to stake out all the launch ramps, Bella devised a plan to have a police harbor unit go out in the Sound with a drone. They could fly it over any boat that fits the criteria."

"Great idea! Kudos to Bella!"

"I'll tell her. What kind of boat should we be looking for?"

"Anything trailerable. Probably an outboard up to twenty-five feet or so."

"Okay, I'll let you know when they're active."

"Great, Willy. I appreciate it."

Locating the boat was the biggest hurdle of the investigation, and Bella's plan just might clear it.

While driving, I was still bummed about losing James Dennis as a suspect. I wondered why, after all these years as a detective, I put so much weight on him. *Was it because I wanted to protect Kayla? Was it because he was the only suspect?* Probably the latter. Regardless, I had wasted a tracking device.

However, I did feel good about the cooperation between Willy, Bella, and me. I knew I needed to stay in my lane, though. They could get in deep shit for sharing information with a civilian, and the fact that I was a former cop and a licensed PI meant nothing to the department.

WHILE MIA AND I were having our late afternoon cocktails, I said, "I spoke with Anne Gibbs yesterday about a psychological profile of the killer. During our discussion, she told me not to rule out a couple."

"A couple? How so?"

"She assumes there is a sexual element at play, and it could be a couple playing out a fantasy."

"Murdering someone?"

"The deaths could have been the end result of some kind of abuse or depravity."

"Fascinating. I never imagined detective work could be so interesting."

After sharing our other work experiences for the week, she went into the kitchen to begin dinner while I followed to watch the news on TV. Once again, they announced a special report on the latest murdered nurse to air that evening with Elsa Nordstrom.

Following the same format as the others, we saw a video of Amy as a little girl learning to ride a bicycle with her father, followed by her playing hopscotch in the street with her friends. Next up was her playing the lead role of Annie in an elementary school play, with her mother's voice narrating the segment. There were more images of her dressed up in her mother's clothes with long gloves, a veiled hat, and lipstick. It appeared Amy had a passion for drama.

After a commercial break, Elsa narrated videos of Amy performing in high school plays where she sang and danced. In my uninformed opinion, I saw some natural talent. There were also clips of her singing folk songs while playing an acoustic guitar. Like all the others, the show wrapped up with her attending and graduating from nursing school.

After watching these reels, it was apparent the nurses were just like any other young women, full of ambition, with their entire lives ahead of them—lives cut short by a senseless murder. These cases, put together, had gotten under my skin, and I realized I would not be able to remain dispassionate. I wasn't sure if that was a good thing.

Mia and I went to bed that night feeling horrible for these young women and their families, causing me, once again, to relive my despair from when Hannah was kidnapped.

Friday was hauling day. After breakfast, I headed to the marina, where I'd need to hang around, awaiting my turn to drive the boat onto the travel lift. When I arrived, they told me it would be after lunch before they'd be ready for me. The temperature had dropped, and the wind picked up, so I spent the rest of the morning inside the clubhouse chatting with Vinny and my other dock mates. With another boating season coming to an end, some of us talked about our winter plans, while some spoke of their dreams for the next season.

My time there was a welcome distraction from the murdered nurses. That was until I received a text from Willy informing me that the Harbor Unit had started that day with a police department drone operator. I became hopeful the killer would be caught in the act.

CHAPTER 13

Mia invited Hannah for dinner on Saturday night to celebrate my birthday, which was the following day. We all hugged upon her arrival, and Mia gave her a tour of the house. Hannah gushed about the house and couldn't stop talking about Mia's bathroom.

While Mia was in the kitchen, Hannah and I sat in the living room overlooking the Sound, each with a glass of chardonnay, and watched the sunset over Manhattan. She was captivated by the vivid colors beyond the iconic skyline.

As promised, Mia made lasagna. Her version was meatless, made with just vegetables and cheese. Along with spinach, garlic, and mushrooms, she used zucchini from her garden and, of course, the home-grown tomato sauce. She served it with garlic bread and a salad while I poured some Montepulciano.

Hannah, the lasagna aficionado, loved it. After discussing the food, our conversation shifted to Hannah's work, where she shared with us what she was doing and what she had learned. "I've been assigned to the CEO's office staff, and while I'm the most junior member there, I'm proud to work with him directly." Her blue eyes sparkled as she spoke. While I knew nothing about corporate office hierarchy, it sounded impressive.

After dinner, we took cappuccinos into the living room while digesting our meal, this time overlooking the lights on Long Island. At some point, I was left alone for a minute, and then Hannah and Mia returned, carrying a cake with birthday candles, and sang "Happy Birthday" to me. The cake was dark chocolate with a layer of peanut butter cream, my favorite, as only Hannah would know. After my first bite of the rich, moist cake with gooey filling, I said, "Thanks for remembering, Han. This is fantastic!"

"Of course, Dad. I'll always remember!"

WE SLEPT IN late on Sunday and awoke to a steady rain. In her dressing room, Mia had a coffee maker and a mini-fridge. She made coffee, which we enjoyed in bed before enjoying each other's bodies for the rest of the morning. After going downstairs to eat, I made a fire in the fireplace, and we spent the afternoon cuddled on the couch, warmed by the embers, as the rain ran down the glass in sheets. We made love again, right there in our happy place—it was just one of those days when we couldn't get enough of each other.

"Not bad for fifty-six," she teased. "Happy birthday, lover!"

MONDAY BROUGHT ANOTHER workday with Mia in her library and me at the dining room table, huddled over my laptop and casebook. I went through the book once again, looking for direction. My thoughts returned to the lists from Amy's mother and boyfriend, and the fact that they did not match. I was sure there was a logical explanation, but I couldn't let it go. Not wanting to bother Joan again, I called Gary Leonard, whose phone number was on the list he had sent me.

"Hello?"

"Hi, Gary. This is Dan Burnett. First, my sympathies for your loss, and I want to thank you for the list of Amy's friends you sent over."

"No problem. Is there something else I can do for you?"

"I was wondering if we could meet; I'd like to understand Amy better. I can come to your house if you'd like."

"How about we meet somewhere for coffee?"

"Sure. You pick the time and place."

Pausing momentarily, he asked, "Do you know the Starbucks on Tarrytown Road in White Plains?"

"I'm sure I can find it."

"I can meet you there at 2:00 today."

"That works for me. Thanks, Gary. I'll see you then."

Arriving at Starbucks a few minutes after 2:00, I realized we had not made plans to identify each other. Fortunately, only one guy in the place was close to Amy's age. He was thin and average-height, with a weak attempt at a straggly beard and mustache. He was sitting by the windows, looking at his phone, and reminded me of Shaggy from Scooby-Doo.

"Excuse me, might you be Gary?" I asked, approaching him from behind.

Looking up from his phone, he replied, "Mr. Burnett, right?"

"Yes, thanks for meeting me."

"No problem. What did you want to know about Amy?"

"Can I buy you a coffee? It's time for my afternoon pick-me-up."

"Sure. Regular, please."

When I returned with the coffee, I said, "I'm wondering

why your list of friends didn't have all the names from Mrs. Patterson's list?"

"Really? Who did I forget?"

"Natalie Morgan and Rebecca Yates."

"Well, I didn't include Natalie because she's dead, and the other name, I don't recognize."

"Rebecca Yates. She was one of the nurses with whom Amy had drinks on Friday nights."

"I didn't know those girls."

"Tell me about Amy; what was she like?"

He shrugged. "I don't know, just a regular girl."

"Did she like her job?"

"I guess."

I could see this was going nowhere, but continued, "What did you two like to do together?"

"We liked hanging out at bars."

Becoming impatient with his dumb act, I said, "Listen, I'm trying to find a connection between the murdered nurses. Were there any clubs or groups she belonged to where she may have known the other nurses?"

"Isn't the murderer just some wacko with a fetish?"

"That could be. But that's the easy explanation. It's my job to pursue other possibilities."

"Good luck with that. I think he's just a whack job."

After a sip of coffee, I said, "What do you do for work, Gary?"

"Custom kitchens. I design and install them in all the big homes around here."

"All?"

"Well, many."

Frustrated, I rose from my seat and said, "Thanks for your time," and took my coffee to go.

While returning to Mia's, my frustration turned to anger as I wondered if Gary was as dumb as he led on. While he may have installed kitchens, he didn't appear bright enough to design them, nor have the business savvy to be hired for the big, expensive jobs. But soon a smile came over my face as I imagined kicking his ass—it was only then that I scolded myself for letting him get under my skin.

ANOTHER REPORT OF a missing young woman was in the news the following day. Her name was Melinda Bernardi, and while she wasn't a nurse, she was last seen leaving the Mount Sinai doctors' offices in Scarsdale, where she worked in accounting and records. I saw her parents in tears on TV, telling the reporter they had feared this since the whole nurse thing had started. Her car was found outside a CVS pharmacy between her place of work and her home. I knew the first thing the police would jump on would be the store's security camera video. I hoped there were images of the parking lot that would identify the perp—either an image of his face or his vehicle's license plate.

A few minutes later, I received a call from Elsa Nordstrom. "Hi, Dan. Do you have a minute?"

"Sure, Elsa. How are you today?"

"I'm fine. What do you know about the latest missing woman?"

"Melinda Bernardi? Nothing, I've never heard of her until today."

"You're former NYPD, right?"

"That's right." *So she did research me.*

"Do you have sources within the department?"

"Not really."

"Then how was it that you were at the beach the other day when the body was found?"

"I just happened to be driving through town and followed the police cars."

"I see. Tell me what you know about the others."

I felt like I was being interrogated, and my initial reaction was to clam up, but I also wanted to keep this source open. I said, "Pretty much everything I know, I learned from you."

"Oh, please. Flattery will get you nowhere with me, Dan."

Realizing this would be a transactional relationship, I said, "Well, I have spoken with the parents of the murdered nurses."

"What did you learn from them?"

"Did you know that Amy and Natalie knew each other?" I said, attempting to flip this conversation around.

"No. This is the first time I've heard of a connection between them."

Hearing a change in her tone, I asked, "Is there anything you've discovered that hasn't been on TV?"

"Just that Amy and Laura went to school together."

"That I knew. I've been searching for a connection between any of the nurses."

"Yeah, me too. I guess that's investigation 101," she quipped.

"Let's stay in touch, Elsa. Maybe we can help each other."

"Yes. Maybe we can."

OVER THE NEXT twenty-four hours of media coverage, we learned that Melinda was twenty-one and never wore a uniform. The only video from CVS showed her entering and exiting the store, which confirmed that she was wearing street clothes. Their exterior cameras covered only the front doors and the drive-thru window, so my hopes of identifying the killer from a parking lot view were dashed.

I waited two days before calling the Bernardi family and introducing myself. Like the other families, they were despondent. After expressing my sympathies, I asked for a list of friends. I wasn't quite sure why I kept seeking those—I guess I wanted to keep my spreadsheet up to date, as I had already put so much work into it.

The following day, I loaded Melinda's list of friends into the program and discovered a new connection to Amy Patterson and Rebecca Yates. Sitting back in my chair, I realized a pattern had begun to form after all. Three of the missing nurses knew Amy Patterson. And two other friends, Rebecca Yates and Linda Stein, knew some of them. Yet, they didn't all go to the same school or work in the same place.

However, they were similar in age and body type. A youthful body type that I knew to be attractive to most men: not too heavy and not too thin. I started a new list to identify their characteristics, noting whether they were similar or dissimilar. When I finished the list, I emailed it to Willy, hoping he could add to it from his knowledge. Later that day, he called.

"Thanks for sending over your work, Dan."

"Does any of it jive with your information?"

"It does. Each of the women fits the same profile. Between this list and your spreadsheet, every common link appears to go through Amy Patterson. Without her, no one would have known each other, including Rebecca and Linda, the friends among the living."

"The one exception is Kayla Mateo, who only knew Natalie and Laura."

"Yeah. There's that," Willy conceded. "I was referring to the deceased."

"You're right. All the deaths revolved around Amy. Have you had any luck so far with the Harbor Unit?"

"Nope. The concept works as far as flying the drone over small boats, but they haven't yet spotted anything of interest."

"I assume this is a daytime-only operation?"

"Yes, it is. No searchlights involved."

"Okay, Willy. Good luck with it."

"Thanks again, I'll share what I can."

I DIDN'T MIND sharing my work with Willy, and I had no illusions that if they caught the guy, he would let me know first. The NYPD would want all the credit, and I'd learn about it on the television news, like everyone else. Since this was no longer a paid job for me, assisting the police had become a hobby, which I enjoyed more than full-time police work with responsibilities and a boss. Although the pay was non-existent, my goal was simply to bring justice and closure to the families involved. Perhaps my contribution would be mentioned after the fact, for whatever that was worth.

I sat down again with the book and my laptop to review what I knew and didn't know—my near-daily ritual. Using the coroner's estimated time in the water of two to four weeks from the earlier cases, Amy's case appeared to fit the pattern. She had been missing for one month and could have been kept alive for a week or perhaps killed and dumped immediately. I felt like I was grasping at straws, trying to make the facts match my theories. From experience, I knew it was time to step back and let the facts come to me.

With every intention of taking a few days off, I slept in, and while lounging around in bed, I decided to make lunch for Mia. After browsing recipes online, I went to the grocery store, bought the makings for a curried chicken salad, and then went to work in the kitchen. After sautéing diced chicken in madras curry, I placed it in the fridge to cool. I mixed diced celery and Granny Smith apples with chopped walnuts and golden raisins in a large bowl. Then, I added mayonnaise and plain yogurt along with the chicken, stirred it together, and returned it to the fridge.

When it was chilled, I cut slices of fresh sourdough bread and mounded them with the curry mixture, before laying a leaf of red lettuce on top, and finishing with another slice of bread.

I set the table and cut the sandwiches in half before I called Mia from her library, hoping she'd be impressed.

She entered the kitchen and exclaimed in surprise, "I smell curry!" After her first bite, I heard, "Oh, Dan, this is delicious! Where did you learn to make it?"

"I'll admit to perusing the Food Network website this morning," I grinned.

"How did you know I love curry?"

"I remembered you raved about it on Martha's Vineyard this summer."

"This is even better. I'll want you to make it again."

After eating, she said, "That was a wonderful lunch, love. And so sweet of you." She kissed me before returning to her library.

A WHILE LATER, I heard from Willy. "Hey, Dan. The Harbor Unit just picked up two guys who were dumping something in the Sound. They say it could have been a body."

"Where are they?"

"They're taking them to the 109th Precinct, near LaGuardia, but they marked the location so a dive team can search the area."

"That's good to hear. Maybe the harbor effort paid off."

"Let's hope. I'll keep you posted, Dan."

WHILE MIA AND I were enjoying a cocktail in our happy place, Willy called back. "The two guys on the boat lawyered up immediately, but they've been ID'd as Vincent D'Tulio and Anthony Pasquale from Queens. They have priors but no jail time. Mostly small-time gang-related stuff from a while back."

"But now they have lawyers?"

"Yeah, they must have stepped up their game. The word is they're involved with an organized outfit."

"Where were they picked up in the Sound?"

"Halfway between Glen Cove and Larchmont."

"That's precisely where I suspect the nurses' bodies were dumped based on my research with NOAA," I said proudly.

"They'll be spending the night at Rikers. We'll know more in the morning after their arraignment."

"Is the dive team onsite yet?"

"They're supposed to be. I'll let you know when I hear anything."

My heart was racing in anticipation of a breakthrough.

CHAPTER 14

At noon the next day, my phone lit up—from caller ID, I knew it was Willy. "So the divers found a body in a burlap sack with a bullet in his head—a rather large body. The Vic was a known wise guy from Jersey."

"Well, that's a whole new kettle of fish. Do you suppose these guys get rid of bodies for hire?"

"That's possible. The prosecutor has an interview scheduled for 2:00 with the attorney present. I'll be there, too. I can get you behind the one-way glass if you want to observe."

"Great. I'll meet you at Rikers at 1:45."

"Do you remember the police entrance?"

"How could I ever forget?"

AFTER EATING A sandwich of leftover curried chicken salad, I headed out, taking the Whitestone Bridge toward Rikers Island Prison. Willy's unmarked Dodge was parked near the entrance among the blue and whites. I parked alongside, and we walked in together.

Willy said, "I have no idea what kind of cooperation we'll get from these guys. If it's a mob attorney, he won't even let them say hello."

After going through a magnetometer and emptying our pockets into a tray, we were led to the interrogation rooms. While Willy went in with the prosecutor and the suspect's attorney, I was seated in the observation room along with the assistant D.A., waiting silently for the prisoners to be escorted in.

I watched through the glass as the guards walked the cuffed and shackled prisoners into the room and began to attach their handcuffs to a hefty ring in the middle of the table. Dressed in prison-issued jeans and T-shirts, their looks matched their names. The attorney said, "Can we forgo the ring? I'm sure my clients will behave themselves."

When the guards looked to the prosecutor, who I recognized as Chuck Daley, he said, "That's okay, fellas. You'll be right outside, correct?"

"Yes, sir," the guards replied in unison before they exited the room.

Chuck Daley began, "This interview is being recorded. Today is October 20, 2024, and we are in an interview room at Rikers Island Prison in New York. It is 2:10 p.m., and Vincent D'Tulio and Anthony Pasquale are present, along with their attorney, Salvatore Sarno, and Detective William Grant of the NYPD. Shall we continue, Mr. Sarno?"

"By all means."

"Thank you. Mr. D'Tulio, what do you know about the deaths of four nurses who were found on the shore of Long Island Sound over the last few months near where you were apprehended yesterday?" the prosecutor asked.

"Nothing."

"Mr. Pasquale, same question."

"Nothing, sir."

"What evidence do you have that my clients had anything to do with those poor nurses?" attorney Sarno asked.

"That's what we're here to determine. But the fact that they were found dumping a body in the Sound, near where the young women were found, makes them obvious suspects."

"I guess that's fair, but I can assure you they had nothing to do with those horrible crimes."

"Again, that's what we're here to determine. Besides our divers finding the body of Fat Tony DelMoro, we have a drone video of your clients dumping his body. Would you like to view that video here now?"

"That's not necessary. I'm sure you'll make it available upon request."

"Certainly, Mr. Sarno. Detective Grant, do you have any questions for the suspects?"

"I do," Willy replied, removing four photos from a file folder. After spreading them out in front of the suspects, he asked, "Do either of you recognize these young women?"

"Aren't those the nurses we saw on TV?" D'Tulio replied.

"They are. Do you two work together?"

They looked at the attorney for his permission to answer. When he nodded, D'Tulio said, "Yes. We have a waste management company, mainly hauling."

"By hauling, what do you mean?" Willy inquired.

This time, Pasquale answered. "We run garbage trucks and dump trucks. Most of our work is hauling to landfills."

"What are you charging my clients with?" the attorney asked.

"Murder. We have yet to determine the degree."

"Murder? How do you know they didn't just find the body in a dumpster?"

"The charge will certainly be more serious than littering, Mr. Sarno."

"I'd like a few minutes alone with my clients."

"That's fine," Chuck said as he and Willy rose to leave the room.

"And shut off the recording and microphone and close the curtain to your spy room."

Chuck did all those things, and then he and Willy joined us in the observation room. "I presume he's having a chat with them about proposing a plea deal," Chuck said.

"Are you considering a plea deal?" Willy asked.

"No freakin' way. We'll bleed these guys for everything they know about their bosses, as well as the crime gripping this city. We'll let them sit in a cell for another night. I'm sure Sarno will argue for bail before the judge in the morning."

With that, Chuck opened the door to wait for the attorney to step outside.

A moment later, he did. "Okay, gentlemen, can we reconvene?"

Chuck and Willy returned to the interview room, raised the curtain, and turned on the microphone and recorder. Chuck announced, "We are recording again."

Attorney Sarno stated, "To save us all a lot of time and effort, if my clients plead guilty to illegal dumping, can we put an end to this charade?"

"You must be joking! That's not going to happen. You can argue bail with the judge in the morning if you'd like."

"Chuck, you're being unreasonable. My clients are hard-working members of society, with families who are worried about them."

"You're aware of their priors, aren't you, Sal?"

"Those were all either dismissed or were misdemeanors."

"Yes, I have the printouts right here," he said, raising a file. "Just the fact that you're representing them indicates this is mob-related."

"Oh, please. I have clients from all walks of life."

"That's nice. I'm happy for you. I can tell you that I'll argue for them to be held without bail."

"All right, we'll see you in court." He turned to his clients and said, "Don't worry, I'll have you out by noon tomorrow."

When Chuck signaled for the guards, D'Tulio and Pasquale sagged in their seats, disappointed to spend another night in a cell, while the rest of us left the building.

When I returned to Mia's, it was well past happy hour, but she had a shaker of Manhattans waiting for me. I brought her up to speed with the day's happenings while we sipped our drinks in our happy place.

"Do you think they had anything to do with the nurses?" she asked.

"I have no idea. Maybe they're the go-to guys for getting rid of bodies, but the spot they dumped the mobster is too close to be a coincidence."

"What are your plans from here?"

"I was planning to take a few days off until this came up. I think I'll resume those plans while Willy and the prosecutor do their thing."

"So, I can have you all to myself for the next few days?"

"You may," I said, pulling her close.

"I have a design due tomorrow, but how about we go to Newport for the weekend?"

"Sounds good to me. I'll try to make a reservation."

"Oh, goodie!" She kissed my cheek before rising to make dinner.

THE FOLLOWING DAY, I drove to the marina to check on Privateer. She was now up on stands, packed in the lot with other boats, and I saw that the shrink wrap had been completed. After climbing aboard and checking on everything, I had lunch with some dock mates at the diner. Later, while driving to Mia's, Willy called.

"Hi, Dan. D'Tulio and Pasquale just made bail. A quarter mil each."

"I assume their boat was searched and tested for prints or DNA?"

"Yup. There was nothing linking them to the nurses."

"What were they charged with?"

"Dumping a human body, a class-E felony. But he's considering adding murder charges if they don't cop to who hired them."

Knowing a class-E carries a four-year sentence, I asked, "What are your thoughts, Willy?"

"I'll try to link them to the nurses. We'll subpoena phone records, etc. You know the drill."

"All right, good luck with it. I'm going away for the weekend to clear my head. Let's touch base Monday."

"You got it. Enjoy yourself!"

Mia and I had sailed Privateer to Martha's Vineyard over the summer, and Newport was one of our stops. Her sister Judy met us there, and we had enjoyed a few days of wandering the waterfront, perusing the shops, and dining at many of the restaurants.

After checking into the Castle Hill Inn, where Mia paid for our room, we wandered around the waterfront, visiting our favorite places from the summer. After a late afternoon cocktail at the Black Pearl, we returned to the Inn for dinner overlooking the bay. One might think we'd be tired of looking at the water between Mia's house and my sailboat, but somehow, we never were.

Mia had dressed elegantly in a snug black dress with silver trim and matching heels. Since back in the folds of fashion, she was more daring—her dress full-length but narrow, with a side slit up to her hip revealing a flawless leg. While she usually tried not to draw attention to herself, her beauty couldn't remain hidden when she dressed up. All eyes were on her as we made our entrance—the men envious, and the women jealous.

The dining room overlooked the mouth of Narragansett Bay, and we watched the sailboats return from their day at sea. Some had been racing, and some were arriving from distant places. As darkness crept over the bay, we could see lights all the way out to Point Judith.

After a cocktail, we ordered the chef's six-course tasting menu, which included duck pâté, striped bass, venison, and a dark chocolate mousse with red currants for dessert. Everything was fresh and locally sourced. Each course featured a wine pairing, beginning with Champagne and concluding with Port.

I learned to appreciate food like this from my father, god rest his soul, who was a chef at a French restaurant in Manhattan. This was a splurge meal for me, and I was glad to have logged at least a few paid hours over the last week. I'm sure Mia and her late husband dined like this regularly. But for me, a retired cop on a pension with alimony payments and some part-time income, it was a special night. Regardless, the meal was fabulous.

When we returned to our room, which also had a water view, Mia lit candles and turned off the lights so we could see the stars and pinpoints of light twinkling across the bay. Once my eyes adjusted, I could see Mia had changed into a silk teddy. We sat in an overstuffed chair by the windows, looking out at the night with me wearing boxers and her in my lap. Her scent, although light, was intoxicating, and I began nuzzling her breasts. Gradually, when her nipples were at full attention, I rose with her in my arms and carried her to the bed. It was a night to remember as we made love multiple times, dozing off in between. The first hints of the rising sun peered through the windows as we climaxed together the last time.

Mia must have pulled the drapes at some point because we slept until checkout time. Having missed breakfast, the kitchen staff was kind enough to serve us coffee, juice, and popovers on the patio.

MONDAY, I FELT rested and invigorated, yet anxious to hear from Willy. With Mia working in her library, I spent the morning obsessing over the case book, looking for something I had missed. Just before noon, Willy called.

"How was your weekend, Dan?"

"It couldn't have been better!"

"Good to hear. So, these two guys are definitely tied to the mob. Besides the trash hauling, they run a neighborhood protection scam in Queens, extorting money from local businesses."

"With all the typical threats and consequences, I would imagine."

"Exactly. So far, we haven't found anything linking them to the nurses; no phone calls to Westchester County or any history of them operating there."

"What does your gut tell you, Willy?"

"I think they were getting rid of a rival gang member. Fat Tony's DNA was all over the boat and the trunk of Pasquale's car, so the D.A. has charged them with manslaughter. But we found no evidence or DNA linking them to the nurses."

"So, we're back to square one?"

"I guess so. The Captain's pulling us off and letting the organized crime unit deal with them."

"I get it."

"The Harbor Unit will continue the operation, though, so something might still turn up."

"All right. Thanks for the call, Willy."

"Of course."

I leaned back, took a deep breath, and exhaled. Every time we had a promising lead, it quickly evaporated. While I've certainly had my share of leads that fell through during my career on the force, for some reason, this case felt personal to me.

Discouraged, I recalled what I would have done while with the department: I would have stirred the pot. I decided to reach out to the victims' families one more time. Perhaps they had remembered something helpful, opening a new avenue of investigation for me.

I began with Doug and Cindy Morgan, my original clients. It was Cindy who answered the phone.

"Hello, Mrs. Morgan. Dan Burnett here."

"Do you have news for us?" she asked eagerly.

"I'm sorry, I don't. I was just checking in to see how you two were doing, I mean, with all the other nurses who've turned up."

"It's very upsetting. Doug and I cry every time we hear about another one. We just can't seem to put this behind us—maybe we never will."

Hearing the disappointment in her voice, I scolded myself for making the call. But I tried to make the best of it. "Had either of you heard any of these women's names before?"

"No."

"I wish I had something positive to share with you."

"Thanks for thinking of us, Dan."

Realizing how a call from me might raise false hopes in the families, I reconsidered making the calls altogether. To continue, I'd need to share a positive development, and I thought for a moment how to do that. I tried a different tactic with Laura Kelly's parents.

"Hello, Mr. Kelly?"

"Yes?"

"It's Dan Burnett. This might not be much, but I wanted you to know that the police have assigned more officers and detectives to the case."

"It's about time they put the manpower on it that it deserves."

Feeling better about his reaction, I asked, "How are you and Mrs. Kelly doing?"

"About as good as could be expected. Laura's sister is taking it the worst. She stays in her room all day and hasn't been to school since they found Laura's body."

"Has anything else come to mind that might be helpful?"

"Nothing I can think of. We're just frustrated with the police. You'd think they'd keep us posted on their progress, or maybe they have none."

"Well, their plates are full right now, but I can assure you, they're working on it."

"If you say so. Thanks for the call, Mr. Burnett."

After a similar conversation with Sierra's fiancé, Devan Wolfe, I tried Amy Patterson's mother, Joan. I saved her for last because I wanted to ask about all the nurses that Amy knew. I also hoped to comfort her now that we knew she was gone forever.

"Hello."

"Hi Joan, this is Dan Burnett calling. I wanted to let you know that the police have added more officers and detectives to the case."

"It's about time."

"How are you holding up?"

"Oh, I don't know. I'm still waking up in the morning and saying my prayers at night."

"How well did Amy know the other missing nurses?"

"The only one I met was Natalie. I never heard her speak of the others. The names I sent you were from her phone contacts."

"I see."

"Maybe Gary would know better."

"I spoke with him already. He doesn't seem to know much."

"That's odd—he knows all of Amy's friends."

"Should I try him again?"

"You won't reach him right now; I just saw him drive by towing his boat."

"Excuse me?"

"He's probably going fishing. Amy went with him a few times."

My jaw hung open. After a deep breath, I said, "Thanks for your time, Joan. If you think of anything else, let me know."

It took me a few minutes to calm my racing heart. *Could this be the break we've been looking for?* The fact that Gary Leonard had a boat exactly like the one we're searching for changes everything. I knew I needed to share this with Willy, but after some consideration, I thought I'd first follow up on a few things myself.

Gary told me he'd never met the other nurses. If he was lying, maybe these weren't random snatches after all.

I thought of reaching out to Rebecca or Linda, the friends who were still alive. My first call was to Linda Stein.

"Hello?"

"Hi Linda, this is Dan Burnett; we spoke a few weeks ago."

"Yes. I remember."

"Did you, by chance, ever meet Amy's boyfriend, Gary?"

"As a matter of fact, I did. Amy brought him to one of our Friday night get-togethers over the summer."

"Was it usual for any of you to bring boyfriends?"

"No, absolutely not. These were supposed to be girls' night out—no men. I was a bit pissed."

"I'm just trying to fill in the blanks here, but were any of the other missing nurses there that night?"

"Hmmm. I don't remember who was there that night. Not everybody showed up every time."

"Okay, if something jogs your memory, would you let me know?"

"Sure. I'll try to focus on it."

"Thanks, Linda."

After making some notes, I called Rebecca Yates. When the call went to voicemail, I texted her to contact me. A few minutes later, she did.

"Hello, Mr. Burnett. Sorry, I was on the phone."

"No problem. Thanks for calling back. Please call me, Dan."

"What can I do for you, Dan?"

"I have a question about your Friday night get-togethers: Did you ever meet Amy's boyfriend, Gary?"

"I did. Sometime after the Fourth of July. I remember because Amy told us about watching the fireworks from his boat."

"Do you recall anything else about that night?"

"I remember him showing us his new tattoo. It was some kind of fish jumping out of the water with a hook in its mouth."

"Anything else?"

"Oh yeah—he was hitting on Natalie right in front of Amy. That was weird!"

I pictured that for a moment, and said, "Thanks, Rebecca. You've been a big help."

"Is he a suspect?"

"I have no Idea. I'm just filling in a timeline."

"Okay. Bye, Dan."

After contemplating everything I'd just learned, it was time to call Willy.

"What's up?"

"Do you have a minute?"

"Sure. I'm driving."

"I just discovered that Gary Leonard, Amy Patterson's boy-friend, has a boat he keeps on a trailer."

"No shit?"

I went on to tell him everything I had learned, including that Gary had met some of the other nurses before.

"Do you have an address for Gary Leonard?" Willy asked.

"I don't, but he lives in the same neighborhood as Amy."

"We'll find it."

"Amy's mother thinks he's out on the boat now."

"Good to know. I'll do a DMV check, and we'll try to coordi-nate a search with the local police of all the launch ramps for his vehicle and trailer."

"Keep me posted if you can."

"I will. Thanks for this. It might be the break we've been waiting for."

"Good luck!"

I sat back in my chair, feeling pumped at this new revelation. Now hungry, I went across the foyer and asked Mia if she wanted a sandwich.

"No thanks, love. I'm skipping lunch today."

I guess she's still trying to fit into that dress. I made myself a roast beef sandwich on a Kaiser roll. While my mind reeled, I carefully lay-ered on the meat, sliced fresh tomato, a leaf of lettuce, and spread mayo on the roll before placing it on top. After cutting the sandwich in half, I devoured it in minutes.

I knew Willy would be all over the new information and thought about how the police would proceed if they located the trailer at a launch ramp. They would most likely wait for him to return, then impound everything: the boat, the trailer, and the vehicle. I assumed they would obtain a warrant to search his house and his phone records. There wasn't a judge in the state who would deny a warrant for this case. I monitored the television for the rest of the afternoon and evening, hoping to see Gary's arrest.

It never happened.

CHAPTER 15

A day went by before Willy called.

"Hey, Willy. How did you make out with Gary Leonard?"

"We never found him at any boat ramps, but we coordinated with the Elmsford Police and staked out his house. When he returned with the boat, we executed a search warrant. It turns out he uses a launch ramp in Cos Cob, Connecticut."

"Did anything useful turn up during the search?"

"Forensics went through his house, and we just got the written report back this morning, which is why I waited to call. The only evidence of any nurses being there was Amy. They found a DNA match from a hairbrush and a toothbrush. They also found her fingerprints and a few items of clothing there."

"Nothing else?"

"Nope. There was no dungeon in the basement where he abused the nurses, either."

"So, not enough to make an arrest?"

"That's correct. He has a clean record with no priors. I still think he's good for it, though, so we'll watch him like a hawk."

"I assume you checked the boat for evidence?"

"Yup. It had all been washed down with bleach. He said he does that to get rid of the fish smell."

"Convenient."

"That it is."

"Do you have a tracker on his vehicle?"

"We have trackers on his Toyota pickup and his boat. I shared the boat tracking app with the Harbor Unit. We're also monitoring his cell phone and credit cards. Judge Henry signed a blanket warrant for anything we could think of."

"Good to know. Is there anything I can do that you can't?"

"With this warrant, we seem to have unlimited powers."

"A detective's dream!"

"It sure is."

"Okay, Willy. Thanks for letting me know."

After digesting the call, I felt confident it was only a matter of time before Gary Leonard would be behind bars.

LATER THAT AFTERNOON, I received a call from Linda Stein.

"Hi, Dan. I thought of something else about Amy that was a bit odd."

"I'm all ears."

"Okay, none of this I know for a fact, but I often wondered if Amy and Natalie had a romantic relationship."

"How so?"

"They seemed closer to each other than the rest of us, and I saw them holding hands a few times. It felt like they knew something the rest of us didn't. But when I saw that Amy had a boyfriend, I assumed there was nothing to it."

"I see."

"But then, one night, I saw the three of them together at a frozen yogurt place. They were stoned and making out at a sidewalk table."

"When was this?"

"About a week after Amy brought him to the bar—probably mid-July."

"Interesting. Thanks for sharing this, Linda."

"Maybe it's nothing."

"We'll see."

A LOT HAD happened, and I added it all to the case book for future reference. While noting what Willy had told me about the search of Gary's house, something jumped out at me about his vehicle. He said it was a Toyota pickup.

I leafed back through the pages to the time I was with Kayla Mateo, and she described the pickup that followed her as black and mid-size. The very next day, Frosty referred to it as a Japanese make.

I called Willy again.

"Yes, Dan."

"What color is Gary Leonard's pickup?"

"Black. Why?"

"That matches the description of the vehicle that followed Kayla Mateo home from Westchester Med."

"Refresh my memory of who she is?"

"She's a nurse who knew Natalie Morgan and maybe some of the others."

"Okay."

"Do you have pictures of the truck?"

"I'm sure we do; we took pictures of everything during the search."

"Send them to me, please. I'll forward it to her for confirmation."

"You'll have them in a few minutes."

"Thanks, Willy."

Willy sent two pictures, and I texted them to Kayla, asking if this was the vehicle that followed her. Five minutes later, she called. "That's the truck, Dan. I remember the shape of the fenders, and with that big trailer hitch, there's no doubt in my mind."

"Thanks—I'll keep you informed."

"Please do."

I called Willy back. "We have a positive ID on the truck."

"Good. Send me all the info for this woman. We'll follow up."

"You got it."

"Thanks, Dan."

I typed out an email with everything I knew about Kayla Mateo, including that she had previously spoken to Detective Matt Frost at the 49th Precinct, and sent it to Willy. I also emailed Frosty a copy that included the pictures.

THE NEXT DAY was November 1st. Two months had gone by since I discovered Natalie Morgan's body. Today was also the day the body of Melinda Bernardi washed ashore on East Island Beach, along the north shore of Long Island, near Glen Cove.

The DNA match was completed within hours because the forensics team was already waiting with a sample provided by Melinda's parents. By mid-afternoon, the media were all over it, reigniting the panic around New York. I assumed that within a few days, Elsa Nordstrom would do another special report.

From everything I knew, I agreed with Willy that all the cases revolved around Amy Patterson. Two of the five deceased nurses knew her, as did Amy herself. Only Sierra Swan and Melinda Bernardi were outliers.

I called Linda and Rebecca again to ensure they had no contact with Sierra or Laura. They both confirmed they didn't know them.

WILLY CALLED TO tell me Captain Alexander appreciated the information and thought Kayla's account of the truck following her would add to the eventual list of charges against Gary Leonard. However, it was not yet enough to issue an arrest warrant. I then told him about the possible tryst among Amy, Natalie, and Gary, as reported by Linda Stein.

"Interesting," Willy said. "That's a new wrinkle."

"I thought so. Today's discovery of Melinda Bernardi marks the fifth in two months. I don't recall any other stalker case where the perp was that aggressive."

"I agree. They're usually months apart, not weeks."

"Am I correct that we have no reported missing nurses that have yet to be found?"

"That's correct, but there's possibly one more we've kept to ourselves."

"Can you tell me about it?"

After a moment, he said, "Okay, but this can't get out."

"Got it."

"There's another case from June. It was reported before the others, and since she wasn't a nurse and wasn't found in the water, we didn't initially make the connection. Some hunters found the remains of a young woman in the woods near the Muscoot Reservoir in Katonah. We learned later that she was in the nursing program at SUNY Westchester in Ossining."

"That's where Amy and Laura went to school."

"Exactly. Look, a lot of what we know, we learned from you. How about I talk to my captain about bringing you into the loop?"

"I remember Captain Alexander from Mia's brother's case."

"That's why he might consider letting you in."

"I'm happy to help in any way I can."

"Okay, I'll let you know if we have that conversation."

At 4:00 that afternoon, Mia wandered out of her library and put her arms around me. I'd been busy at the dining room table all day. When she leaned over my back and kissed me on the side of my neck, I got a hint of her scent—*Mmm.*

"How about making us a cocktail, love?"

"That sounds good," I said, sliding out of my chair.

She followed me into the kitchen and put some cheese and crackers on a plate while I shook up some Cosmos. After pouring, I followed her to our happy place, where she sat on her legs beside me on the couch.

While talking about each other's work week and nibbling on cheese, she said, "How about we take a ride to Pierre's for dinner tonight? My treat."

Pierre's was a favorite romantic place of ours. We went there after we said *"I love you"* to each other for the first time.

"That sounds wonderful. We haven't been in a while."

"I'll need to bathe first," she said.

"And I need to shower and shave."

"Shall we shower together?"

"Are you sure there's room for both of us?"

She punched me in the arm and laughed, rising to head upstairs. Her shower was big enough for half a dozen people.

I shaved before joining her, and we began kissing. It wasn't long before I became aroused, and she remarked, "Oh my. I'll take care of that later," and hopped out of the shower.

Mia could be playful, and I loved her for it. I knew she wanted to let the anticipation build throughout the evening.

PIERRE'S WAS AN old stone house in the country that had been converted into a restaurant. As the name suggests, they served French cuisine. After parking, we approached the front door through a manicured garden with ivy growing up the face of the building. There were multiple intimate dining rooms inside, and if it wasn't too busy, you could have a room to yourself. Fortunately, that was the case that night.

We sat at a formal table for two in the middle of a small dining room with a starched white tablecloth and napkins. The lighting was dim, and the place settings were formal. There was more silverware than I knew what to do with, and the stemware appeared to be crystal, at least to my untrained eye. Around us were a few more similar tables, all vacant, with heavy drapery swagged at the windows.

Mia looked beautiful, as always. She wore a snug red dress with fitted shoulders and a neckline that plunged to her navel. I wondered if this daring dress was what she'd been trying to fit into. With her hair done up on top of her head and a hint of makeup, she wore diamond earrings and a matching diamond pendant on a long, delicate chain that rested in her cleavage, leading my eyes there. She was indeed trying to torture me that evening.

Mia started with a salad, and I had escargot. We shared a pot of bouillabaisse for our entrée, accompanied by crusty bread and a bottle of Pouilly-Fuissé. She was especially talkative that evening and led the discussion, speaking first about food and then about fashion.

With each movement of her head, light reflected off her dangling earrings, accenting her long, tapered neck, while the pendant danced between her breasts. Mesmerized, I again felt the beginnings of arousal and quickly refocused on my meal. Dinner was marvelous, and we sat awhile longer to finish the wine. When we returned to her house, she led me upstairs, and after pulling back the covers and lighting candles, she slipped off the fabulous dress and rewarded me for my patience.

WHILE MIA WAS preparing for a day in the city, I ate breakfast in the kitchen while watching TV. About halfway through my bowl of fruit and yogurt, there was breaking news: Another young woman had gone missing after arriving at work that morning at a real estate office in New Rochelle. Elsa Nordstrom stood beside the possible victim's car in the parking lot and told us this twenty-six-year-old woman, Ariana Alonzo, was never seen entering the building. The last person to see her was her husband, Miguel, when she left for work at eight a.m.

While the missing nurse story had been the focus of the New York area for the past few months, and this event sounded similar, she was not a nurse. Nevertheless, the media resumed their frenzy. It had been only a few hours, and there could be plenty of explanations for her brief disappearance, but I must admit, it sounded like another one.

Before Mia left for the day, she paused to kiss me and saw what I had been watching.

"Another one?"

"Perhaps, but this one's not a nurse; she's a real estate agent."

"Oh my. Well, I've got to go. Have a good day, love."

"You too, sweetheart."

A FEW MINUTES later, I called Elsa.

"Good morning, Dan. Did you see me on TV?"

"I did. So this one's not a nurse?"

"Right, she's a real estate agent. Her coworkers are wondering if she's with a client."

"So she might not have been abducted after all?"

"Her coworkers have been calling her cell all morning. She doesn't answer."

"Would it be typical for her to ride with the client?"

"Not likely. They said she always drives."

"Anything else you can share?"

"There's nothing else I know."

"Okay, I'll stay tuned."

"Good. The network will be happy to hear that."

LATER THAT DAY, after Mia and I enjoyed our late-afternoon Manhattans, I monitored the news for anything more on the latest missing woman while she prepared dinner. Elsa was back on the screen, speaking with Miguel Alonzo, the victim's husband. They were at the front door of his modest suburban home, and he was bouncing a baby boy in one arm. Miguel appeared to be in a trance, like a deer caught in headlights. I felt terrible for him that Elsa thought it necessary to invade his home just hours after his wife's disappearance.

While she asked him all the usual questions, he did his best to answer before the infant started to fuss. Finally, he excused himself and closed the door. Elsa signed off, just like any other assignment, as the station went to commercial.

THE FOLLOWING MORNING, she was back on the screen, speaking to a police spokesman and asking if they had any leads. He confirmed that Ariana had not returned home overnight, and she asked him if they thought this was related to the missing nurse cases. He artfully ended the questioning without a definitive answer.

With a new victim, I reviewed the case book to see how this case might fit in with the others. When I reached the common friend spreadsheet, I thought adding Ariana Alonzo's list would be helpful, but I was hesitant to contact the husband this soon after his wife's disappearance. And after watching Elsa's question him, I decided to wait at least another day.

My phone rang later that afternoon.

"We brought Gary Leonard in for an interview today," Willy announced.

"How did that go?"

"He played it calm, cool, and collected with Bella, but got squirrelly when I entered the room. When it was all done, we didn't learn very much. But listen, Captain Alexander would like you to come in for a meeting. Can you make it tomorrow?"

"Sure, anytime."

"How about 11:00?"

"I'll be there."

CHAPTER 16

While getting dressed the next day, I prepared for the meeting with Captain Alexander by reviewing the book. I wanted all the facts fresh in my mind, but I brought the book along as backup.

When I arrived at the 50th Precinct, the desk sergeant notified Willy, and he escorted me back to his office, where I was greeted by his partner, Bella. We hadn't seen one another recently, but had worked together on Mia's brother's case. I noticed she was even more muscular than I remembered.

We chatted briefly before Willy called his captain and told him I was there. We walked a few doors down to the end of the hall, where Captain Alexander welcomed us. He was also a Black man, dressed in full uniform, with stripes on his sleeves and medals on his chest, and he wore a neatly knotted tie. Willy and Bella were in plain clothes like me.

After shaking hands, he said, "It's good to see you again, Dan. Willy tells me you've been quite helpful with the nurse cases."

"Thank you, Captain. Natalie Morgan's parents hired me briefly, but after a week, I didn't find enough to justify my employment. Since then, I've stayed curious and done more investigating on my own."

"Yes, that's what Willy told me. We'd like to bring you back in as we did before; nothing official and no pay," he chuckled.

Smiling, I said, "I understand. I'd love to see this to its conclusion."

"All right then. Willy, you and Bella can share our work with Dan, just so long as it's clearly understood that it remains confidential, and any resolution goes through this precinct."

The three of us nodded and returned to their office. Bella was the first to speak, "We've been considering your theory that maybe these are not random nurse stalking cases. In the earlier case where the woman was found in the woods, the cause of death was strangulation. The coroner had more to work with because she wasn't in the ocean for a month, and it wasn't until we focused on Amy that we found the link to the nursing school."

"And now, with the latest being a real estate agent, the nurse angle is looking shakier by the day," I stated.

"Exactly."

"What do you guys make of the possible relationship between Natalie, Amy, and Gary?" I asked.

"Threesomes happen all the time. They don't usually lead to murder," Willy replied.

"Have you asked the coroner if he can rule in or out if the others were strangled?"

Willy and Bella glanced at each other before Bella answered. "No. I'll do that right now. But that may explain the broken neck vertebrae."

While Bella was on the phone, I asked Willy, "Can you tell me more about Gary's interview yesterday?"

"He's a pretty cool customer. He acts like he's not too bright, but seems to have an answer for everything. I think he's a lot smarter than he wants us to believe. We recorded the interview. If you'd like to watch it. It runs about an hour."

"I would."

When Bella hung up, she said, "He's going to call me back. They said he's up to his elbows in someone's chest at the moment."

Willy and I gave her a sour look. "Thanks for sharing," Willy said, his tone dripping with sarcasm.

"Where can I watch the recording?" I asked.

"Right here on my computer," Willy said. "I'll set it up."

While he was doing that, Bella announced, "It's lunchtime. We usually get take-out from next door. Do you want something?"

"Sure. How about chicken salad on whole wheat and coffee?"

"They'll have that," she said.

I began watching Gary's interview while they went next door.

As it started, Gary seemed relaxed. He sauntered into the room and sat back in the chair, slouched with his legs extended wide, confident that he could handle whatever would come. Bella sat adjacent to him and began. He claimed he didn't know anything about the nurses' disappearances, and told Bella that he loved Amy and was crushed when she disappeared. He admitted to knowing Natalie and said she had visited his house with Amy. Gary told Bella he didn't know the other women but conceded he might have met them at a Friday night bar session Amy had taken him to.

It was about that time that Willy and Bella came back with lunch. I paused the recording while I ate my sandwich, and they ate salads with grilled chicken on top. If you want to look like Willy and Bella, eat only protein and veggies.

When I resumed watching the recording, Willy joined me. Anytime Bella asked Gary about anything specific, he claimed to know nothing about it—the same dumb act I'd witnessed at Starbucks. The interview was going nowhere until Willy entered the room wearing a snug black T-shirt, his muscles bulging, with his badge on a chain around his neck. He sat across from Gary.

Watching it on the screen showed how quietly intimidating Willy was, and Gary grew more uncomfortable. He began wiggling his foot and shifted in the chair a few times. His voice became weaker while answering Bella's questions.

"Have you ever gone for frozen yogurt with Amy and Natalie?"

Pausing, I could see his mind turning, wondering how much the police already knew. Gary answered, "Maybe, I don't recall."

"Were the three of you involved romantically?" Bella asked.

Again pausing, "I never kiss and tell," he snickered weakly.

Willy gave him a look that would strike fear into anyone. As the interview wound down, Willy asked Gary for his cell phone. Initially reluctant to turn it over, he complied when Bella presented the warrant. Once the phone was in Willy's hands, he asked for the password to open it. Gary froze for a moment, afraid of what would be found, I was sure. But he grudgingly told him the four numbers, and Willy logged in. As Willy escorted him out, I noted that Gary seemed dispirited, and his pace was lethargic, unlike when he had walked in. I didn't think we learned anything useful, but my gut told me he was guilty of something.

While Willy and I watched the interview, Bella compared the phone records of Gary, Amy, and Natalie. She copied and pasted them into a spreadsheet, just as I had done with the names. When finished, she announced, "Amy made and received calls from both of them, but

Gary and Natalie never called each other. Oh, and Gary keeps the location function turned off on his phone, so we don't know where he's been."

Bella told us her next mission was to go through their internet use for common searches and websites. None of this was a breaking revelation; it was simply a standard police practice of extracting the most information possible from the available research.

She had seized Gary's hard drive while executing the search warrant and had been given Amy and Natalie's laptops by their parents. I didn't envy the task ahead of her, although she told me they had new software to help sort through the data. We spent another hour together going through what-ifs before I left with a copy of the file on Olivia Wilder, the student nurse found in the woods in June.

I SAT AT the table reviewing the new file with my morning coffee. There was already a list of Olivia's friends and contacts, along with her class schedule, and she had no previous brushes with the law. After loading her list of friends into my spreadsheet, I saw nothing in common with anyone except Amy.

While on my second cup, Willy called.

"Bella may have caught a break with the internet records. Amy, Gary, and Natalie had all visited a website based on BDSM and other atypical sexual interests."

"You mean kinky stuff?"

"Yup. Each of them searched for erotic asphyxiation."

"That's choking and strangulation?"

"Correct. The in-vogue term is 'breath play.' There have been deaths reported of people hanging themselves while masturbating."

"Well, that's a whole new twist to our case."

"For sure. I emailed you a link to the website."

"Thanks. We'll talk later."

Before going to the website link, I Googled erotic asphyxiation. The explanation I read described how reducing oxygen to the brain could increase the intensity of orgasm in both males and females. Deeper clinical explanations of the physiology behind the practice were available, but it was all over my head. I was reminded of the wonder of modern technology that allowed me to find an answer to a question like this instantly. Of course, the same technology enables these websites to exist, and the people who use them to pursue their kinks.

I spent the next hour on the BDSM website. There were graphic pictures of all kinds of sex acts, some I'd never imagined, and some were shocking. When you clicked on a picture, a new menu opened, leading to more variations. There were links to shop for pornography, erotic toys, and links to personal ads. When I typed in "breath play," the first picture I saw was a naked young woman sitting on what looked like a saddle with a noose around her neck. There were similar pictures of well-endowed young men seated in a chair masturbating, also with a rope around their necks. When I clicked on them, more links opened—it appeared to be endless. I saw pictures of restrained women in the throes of orgasm with hands around their necks—both male and female hands.

When I got to the personal ad section, there were listings for hooking up with other people who were into various kinks. You could search by gender, location, and kink. When I clicked on one, I was led to a mailbox within the site. If you wanted to hook up with that person, you left a message for them to contact you. You could leave a phone number, an email address, or another mailbox on the site, for which you had to sign up and provide a credit card to be billed $99 monthly.

I sat back, took a deep breath, and tried to process all I'd seen. I was amazed by this whole other world, which I knew nothing about and had certainly never thought would be so openly displayed on the internet. The website was well-produced, indicating that it must be a lucrative business with a large customer base. Realizing I was out of my element here, I called Anne Gibbs—maybe she could help me understand it all.

"Hello, Doc. Dan Burnett calling."

"Hey, Dan. Have you had any luck with the murdered nurses?"

"Well, that's the reason for my call. Maybe they weren't murdered because they're nurses—they may have been into erotic asphyxiation."

"Breath play?"

"Yes. I guess that's what they're calling it now. What do you know about it?"

"Nothing, really. That's not my area of expertise."

"Okay. Do you know someone who could help me?"

"I'll text you the contact info for a colleague who specializes in sexual diversity."

"Wonderful. Thanks, Doc."

"Anytime. Good luck with it."

ANNE CONNECTED ME with Melanie Abraham, whom I immediately called.

"This is Melanie."

"Hello, Melanie. My name is Dan Burnett; I'm a private investigator. Anne Gibbs suggested I contact you."

"Yes, Mr. Burnett. What can I do for you?"

"I'm hoping you can explain 'breath play' to me."

"I can do that. Would you like to schedule an office visit?"

"Sure, the sooner, the better."

"Does 3:00 today work for you?"

"Yes, thanks! I have your address."

"See you then, Mr. Burnett."

IT WAS LUNCHTIME, and I heard Mia in the kitchen. I wandered in and saw her preparing a big bowl of salad. As I hugged her from behind, she said, "I'm making enough for both of us. Do you want to join me for lunch?"

"Sure. It looks good."

While we ate, I told her about the sexual turn the case had taken.

"Kinky nurses," she said. "Isn't that every man's fantasy?"

"Well, I prefer kinky fashion designers, but I see what you're saying."

Smiling, she said, "Does this help to narrow the investigation?"

After considering her question, I said, "Actually, it sends us off in a whole new direction. I no longer see a definitive connection to nurses."

"Maybe nurses are kinkier than other people."

"Could be. I'll have to look into that."

MIA PUT THE plates in the sink when we finished our salads and gave me a quick kiss before returning to her library. I, of course, went back on the internet to research the sex lives of nurses. There were all kinds of hearsay and opinions that nurses were more sexually active than other people. However, as I got deeper into it, I saw clinical studies showing no difference from the general population.

One study showed that while they had more partners at a younger age, the numbers balanced out by age twenty-five. From the data, there was also no difference between genders. Besides being amazed at the information available on the internet, I chalked this up as another dead end.

WHILE RIDING THE train into Manhattan for my appointment with Melanie Abraham, I still pictured all the murdered young women as nurses and chided myself for clinging to that image. My investigation would surely be handicapped if I weren't viewing it with an open mind.

Melanie's office was in a professional building near Grand Central Station, shared by other psychiatrists and psychologists. When Melanie greeted me, I saw an attractive woman in her forties, expensively dressed with fashionably styled dark hair, perfect makeup, and tortoiseshell glasses, all adding to her professional appearance. When she led me into her inner office, I saw her diplomas and other accolades mounted on the wall behind her desk. The one in the center, issued by Columbia University, read "Doctor of Psychiatry." I thought this might be an expensive appointment.

She sat behind a large piano-black desk and gestured for me to sit opposite in a comfortable winged-back chair. "So, Dan, you want to know more about breath play?" she asked.

"Yes. I'm investigating the recent nurse murders, and it's taken a new twist."

"Do you mean the murders all over the news for the last few months?"

"That's right. There are indications the cause of death may be erotic asphyxiation, and I need to understand it."

"Well, we're seeing more interest in the practice lately. Let me start with a textbook explanation: Breath play is an activity related to bondage and discipline, dominance and submission, sadism and masochism—commonly referred to as BDSM. Like most of those practices, it's motivated by power dynamics, curiosity, pleasure from risk or panic, trusting one's partner, and the release of endorphins. For some, the mere thought of being choked causes sexual arousal. However, while most BDSM kinks do not result in permanent injury, erotic asphyxiation can be fatal."

"What pleasure do they get out of it?"

"Studies show that people into breath play have a fantasy view of the practice and believe it heightens the feeling of pleasure during orgasm. And clinically, endorphins kick in when the oxygen supply is restored."

"Why the sudden popularity?"

"I suppose because films and books have romanticized it. Human interest in sexual kinks relates to mainstream views and fantasies. Many find it sexy to try something new, and it's become more common due to pornography and nonbinary relationships."

"My investigation has led to websites where people are seeking it out. Can it really be that mainstream?"

"I'm not sure mainstream is the correct word, but there are certainly enough people involved who'd want to connect on websites."

"Is it thrill seeking, like jumping out of an airplane?"

"Yes, in a way it is, but on a sexual level. I don't think people orgasm while hanging from a parachute," she chortled.

After a momentary pause, I asked, "Is there anything else I should be looking into?"

Reaching into a drawer, she removed some pages stapled together. After passing it across the desk, she said, "Here's a clinical study on the practice. It goes into more depth than I did today if you want to know more."

"Thank you for your time today, Melanie. You've been a big help."

"Good. There will be no charge for the appointment. I'll consider it a professional courtesy, or maybe my civic duty."

By the time I arrived at Mia's, it was happy hour. She was wrapping up her day when she heard me shaking cocktails and entered the kitchen.

"How does a Martini sound, sweetheart?"

"Perfect!" she said, reaching her arms around my waist and resting her head on my back. "How was your day?"

"I learned more than I ever wanted to know about breath play."

"Let's take these to our happy place, and you can tell me all about it."

We did, and after I told her everything I had learned, she said, "I still don't think I'd want to be choked during sex."

"That's good. I don't plan on choking you," I laughed.

CHAPTER 17

The following day, I returned to the website, curious to see if it made any more sense after reading Melanie's information. I browsed more pictures and discovered that what many of the women were sitting on wasn't a saddle at all, but something called a Sybian. On the page was an ad for the device, and I learned it was a powerful sex toy for women to ride on that had a motorized phallus and vibrator on top. The ad claimed it would deliver the best orgasm of your life. Judging by the price, it would have to!

Surprised by all this, I called Willy.

"Good morning, Dan."

"Hi, Willy. I'm on the BDSM website again. I've heard stuff like this existed, but I always thought it was underground somehow. That website is right out there for anyone to see."

"Yeah, there's some kinky stuff out there. Bella found charges to Amy and Gary's accounts for this website from their credit card records. Amy was billed for four months starting in May, and Gary's first charge was in August, with another in September."

"I suppose we'll need to get the credit card records for all of them."

"Yeah, Bella and I are working on that now."

"So, are we giving up the nurse stalker theory?"

"Not necessarily, but we need to chase this down for the moment. I informed Captain Alexander about all this, and he said he'll need to share it with the Chief. He might assign this to the sex crimes unit, but the Captain wants us to continue until told differently."

"Yeah, I remember how it is. I should tell you about a discussion I had with a shrink yesterday."

"Have you gone off the deep end, Dan?" he laughed.

"Maybe," I chuckled. "No, this was someone who specializes in sexual diversity. She explained why people are into erotic asphyxiation and what they get out of it."

"Do tell."

After relaying everything Melanie had told me, Willy said, "You know, if people didn't do shit like this, we'd be out of a job."

With the website still open, I went to the personal ads and searched for listings in the New York area, finding dozens. After going through them, one caught my eye: a female in her twenties who claimed to be a nurse who was into erotic asphyxiation. I still wasn't sure what being a nurse had to do with it; maybe it led one to believe she was caring, or that they would be safe.

I took a screenshot of the listing and texted it to Bella with the caption, "Could this be Amy?"

Ten minutes later, Bella called. "I responded to that listing yesterday—we'll see if I hear anything back."

"What about getting a subpoena for account records from the website?"

"I already looked into it; they're based in China."

"So much for that. What else is going on?" I asked.

"Do we know how long Amy and Gary had been together?"

"I don't. Shall I ask her mother?"

"Sure. She doesn't seem willing to speak with us."

"Okay. I'll let you know."

"Thanks."

I made the call. "Good afternoon, Joan. Dan Burnett calling."

"Hello, Dan. How are you today?"

"Okay. How are you holding up?"

"I'm all right, I guess."

"Can I ask how long Gary was Amy's boyfriend?"

"Well, she knew him from the neighborhood since elementary school, but I think their first date was the Fourth of July this year. He took her out on his boat to see the fireworks, and they became inseparable after that."

"Does he live in that house alone?"

"Yes. His parents died in a car accident several years ago; the house was left to him."

"So, no roommates or friends?"

"I was never there, but Amy didn't mention any."

"Did Gary ever show a wild side or have any trouble with the law?"

"Not that I'm aware of."

"Okay. That's all I have, Joan—thanks."

"Bye, Dan."

I called Bella and filled her in.

"That's interesting," she said. "It fits with a theory Willy and I have. If we assume Amy was bisexual because of her relationship with

Natalie, what if she had hooked up with Olivia Wilder, got carried away with the choking, and dumped her body near the reservoir? Then, when she started dating Gary in July, she turned him on to the asphyxiation thing, and the next time she or they killed someone, they loaded her into his boat and dumped them in the Sound?"

"Well, that's a lot of assumptions, but it sounds like a reasonable theory to me. What about the possibility that Amy accidentally killed herself?"

"Well, it was either that or Gary choked her to death," Bella conceded.

"True. While both theories fit what we know, they're still just theories."

"Exactly. Now we work to prove or disprove them."

"That's really what we do, isn't it?" I said.

"In a nutshell, yes."

"Wait, what about Melinda? She went missing over a month after Amy."

"Maybe Gary was so into it that he found a girl on his own."

"Or through the website," I suggested.

"And now there's Ariana Alonzo."

"That's right. I'll keep your scenario in mind going forward."

"Okay, Dan. We'll talk later."

"Bye, Bella."

Sitting back in my chair, I thought about trying to get a list of Ariana Alonzo's friends. I felt I'd given Miguel adequate time, so I made the call.

"Hello," he answered, sounding tired.

"Mr. Alonzo?"

"Yes?"

"This is Dan Burnett calling. I'm a private investigator working on the missing nurse cases. Might you have a moment to speak with me?"

"Sure."

"First, I'm sorry to hear about Ariana. Have you heard anything hopeful?"

"Nothing," he said over the sound of a fussing child.

"Did she know any of the nurses?"

"No."

"I'm trying to find any link between them. Could you send me a list of Ariana's friends?"

"I could text you a list when my son takes his nap."

"That would be great, Mr. Alonzo."

"Please, call me Miguel, but I don't think this had anything to do with the nurses."

"Why is that?" My curiosity was piqued.

"Ariana had been into some kinky sex stuff lately."

"How so?"

"I'd rather not get into the details with a complete stranger on the phone."

"Miguel, women are dying out there. If you know anything that could prevent another death, wouldn't you want to help?"

"Maybe."

"Look, I can keep what you tell me confidential and still use the information to prevent another young woman from dying."

"Okay, okay. Ariana was into breath play."

"Tell me about it."

"She saw it on the internet and wanted to try it."

"And did you?"

"I tried but couldn't bring myself to hurt her," he said as his voice cracked.

"That's understandable, Miguel—she's your wife and the mother of your child."

"Exactly. But I feared she would look for it elsewhere. Maybe from the website she was on all the time."

"What website was that?"

"Look, I have to tend to my little one. But I'll text you the name along with her friends. Goodbye, Mr. Burnett."

An hour later, I received Miguel's text. The website was the same BDSM site we'd been focused on, and the list of friends contained a dozen names. After loading them into the spreadsheet, there were no matches—Ariana knew none of the nurses.

With Miguel Alonzo's account of his wife's interest in breath play running through my head, I wondered if Devan Wolfe had a similar experience with his fiancée, Sierra Swan. My intuition had told me he knew more than he let on, so I called him.

"Hello?"

"Hi Devan, this is Dan Burnett calling."

"Do you have anything new?"

"Maybe. This may sound like an odd question, but did Sierra ever have an interest in breath play?" Hearing no immediate response, I said, "Devan?"

"Sorry, Dan. Now that you mention it, she did."

"Tell me about it, please."

"This stays between you and me?"

"Absolutely."

"We enjoyed watching porn together occasionally. About six months ago, she showed me some porn where the guy choked the girl during sex, causing a powerful orgasm. This tuned Sierra on, and she wanted me to do it to her. We experimented with it a few times, and she loved it. Over time, she wanted me to do it longer and harder, but I was afraid of hurting her."

"What happened next?"

"She wanted me to hold my hand over her mouth while pinching her nose so she couldn't breathe. I'd never seen her orgasm so intensely. Then she tried it on me. While it increased her excitement, it didn't do much for me. Certainly not like it did to Sierra."

"Do you know if she ever viewed BDSM websites?"

"Not that I'm aware of."

"Thanks for sharing this with me, Devan. This may be helpful to the investigation."

"So, you're working on it again?"

"For now, I'm assisting the police."

"I'd still like a piece of this guy, Dan."

"I know. I'll keep you posted."

THE FOLLOWING MORNING, I heard from Willy. "Last night, we tracked Gary to Lake Mahopac. He spent the night and is now heading back down the Taconic State Parkway."

"Interesting. Is this the first time he's left the house?"

"We're not sure. We had some problems with the tracking software until this week."

"What are your plans?"

"We're working to identify the address where he spent the night. Maybe that will give us some direction."

"Is he aware you're tracking his pick-up?" I asked.

"We didn't tell him, but he might have guessed it."

I told Willy about my communication with Miguel Alonzo and Devan Wolfe. We chatted for a while about how the asphyxiation kink had become the focus of our investigation.

"I'll keep you posted about Gary," Willy said.

THIS WAS ONE of Mia's days in the city, so I rummaged through the fridge and found some leftover pot roast to make a sandwich at lunchtime. I ate it while watching the news on TV, and just as I was finishing, Willy called back.

"It appears Gary Leonard owns a house on Lake Mahopac," he said.

"Another twist."

"Yeah. We reviewed the tax records online, and his family had owned the house for several years. We'll get a search warrant—do you want to go with us?"

"Sure. Let me know when, and I'll meet you there."

An hour later, he texted me the address and said the local cops would meet us there at 3:00. According to Google Maps, my drive from Mamaroneck would be up the Hutchinson River Parkway and take forty-five minutes. Before I left, I texted Mia that I might be late for dinner.

I arrived right after Willy and Bella, and two Mahopac cops awaited us. The house was a typical ranch style with dark brown vertical siding. One of the locals easily jimmied the lock, and we went inside. At first glance, nothing seemed out of the ordinary. We wandered through the kitchen and out to the back deck, where there was a view of the lake and the other homes along the shore. Most had docks and boats, as did this one, and we saw lawn chairs around a fire pit—a perfect family place to toast marshmallows.

After looking through the kitchen, we went down the hall to the bedrooms and heard muffled whimpers from a room at the end. Bella opened the door to find a young woman bound to the bed by each limb to the four corner posts with rough manila rope. Her eyes were wide with fear, she had a ball gag strapped in her mouth, and was naked except for a skimpy tank top. The room reeked of sex.

Bella draped a towel over the young woman's midsection while Willy untied her. Looking around, I saw a Sybian in the middle of the floor with a leather collar hanging over it from a chain bolted to the ceiling. A floor-to-ceiling rack was bolted to one wall with handcuffs and padded restraining devices attached. On the dresser were vibrators, dildos, whips, and other things I couldn't identify.

Once she was untied and had the gag removed, the fear I had seen in her eyes had turned to tears. I'd seen a lot in my thirty years with the NYPD, but this one was tough. Especially the woman's age—she was just a girl, younger than Hannah.

Willy, I, and the Mahopac cops left the room so Bella could tend to the girl. We gathered in the living room while Willy called his Captain, and one of the Mahopac cops called his superior. I overheard them describing what we'd walked into, and from Willy's side of the conversation, it sounded like Captain Alexander was preparing to have Gary Leonard arrested.

A few minutes later, Bella and the now fully dressed young woman walked out of the room and crossed the hall into the bathroom. When they came out, Bella took her to the kitchen and found a bottle of water in the refrigerator for the girl, who was still sobbing. She kept her head down out of embarrassment, avoiding eye contact, raising it only to gulp the water. Bella told us her name was Jenifer Jordan. The local cops looked at each other and said she was only nineteen and had been reported as a runaway the previous day.

After a few moments, the locals determined she would be brought to the local hospital for a rape kit and then be turned over to her parents. Bella offered to stay with Jenifer until her parents arrived. Once they were gone, Willy and I hung out in the driveway and talked about our next steps while the neighbors next door watched us from the other side of a hedge.

"This is well outside the NYPD forensic team's jurisdiction, and I doubt the locals have their own," I said.

"No way. I'll need to call the Staties again."

He called his contact at the State Police and asked them to send their team. When finished with the call, he read a text and said, "Captain Alexander sent a SWAT team to Gary's house with a warrant for his arrest."

After checking the tracking app on his phone, Willy added, "Gary's truck is in his garage. Hopefully, he'll be in a cell at the 50th Precinct by the time I return."

When Willy went to pick up Bella, I headed for Mamaroneck. The day's events began to sink in while I drove. A lot had transpired, most of it disturbing, and I still wondered when and where we would find Ariana Alonzo. When I texted Mia with my ETA, she replied that she'd have a cocktail waiting for me.

Mia's smiling face brought me joy and distracted me from the ugliness I had just witnessed. After a hug and a kiss, we sat in our happy place, and I told her about it. Her mouth hung open as I described what we found in that bedroom in Mahopac. She was astonished by my story and said, "That sounds like something from a horror movie."

"Definitely. The fear I saw in her eyes will haunt me for a long time."

Later, after another delightful meal with Mia, I received a call from Willy. He told me that Gary had split before the SWAT team arrived and assumed the neighbors in Mahopac had tipped him off. His truck was still in the garage, but they confirmed he had taken an Uber to LaGuardia and were now waiting to hear from the airlines about his flight.

I was still shaken when Mia and I crawled into bed that night, and found comfort in holding her. What always got to me was how human beings could treat one another, although I found some solace in knowing we had probably saved a life. I assumed the case would now be in the hands of the FBI.

CHAPTER 18

While watching the morning news, I saw the lake house in Mahopac swarming with reporters. After revealing the homeowner's name, they reported that a young woman, a girl actually, was found bound and gagged in the house. I was pleased to see they withheld her name.

Elsa was there, and I watched her speculate that this was related to the missing nurses. She told us the Mahopac police would make a statement at 9:00. While I was having my second cup, Mia joined me in the kitchen, already dressed for the day.

"Good morning," I said

"Good morning, love. Is this the scene from the lake house?"

"It is. They're already linking it to the nurse murders."

"Is that your girl, Elsa?"

Taken aback by Mia's inference, I looked at her and raised my eyebrows, "Would you stop, please?"

"Sorry. Are they releasing names?"

"Just the owner of the house, Gary Leonard. They usually withhold the victim's name for sex crimes. The police will be addressing the media in half an hour."

"So, we're done with nurse murders?"

"It sounds like it—I'm sure this is the guy."

The same two officers I met the day before had gathered in front of the cameras in the driveway, along with the Chief of Police, who was the first to speak.

"Yesterday, we were notified by the NYPD of a search warrant for this residence. These two fine officers, Detective Clemens and Officer Kowalski, found the young woman restrained in a bedroom. She's now at home with her parents, and we ask that you respect their privacy. I can also report that a State Police forensics team was in the house most of the night gathering evidence. I can take some questions now."

At least a dozen reporters shouted questions, squeezing to the front to be called on. As the Chief recognized one reporter, she asked if the young lady was a nurse.

"No, she was not," he clarified. "But the NYPD executed the warrant in relation to those cases."

Another asked, "Had this young woman been sexually abused?"

"We can't confirm that at this time."

"Who and where is the owner of this house?"

"The legal owner of this house is Gary Leonard, and his whereabouts are unknown at this time. I can assure you every police department in the state is looking for him."

When they began asking for details about the young woman's condition and identity, the Chief ended the interview.

As the scene wrapped up, Mia went into her library to begin her workday, and I texted Willy to ask if he'd like me to notify the families of the murdered nurses. A moment later, he called.

"Hey, Dan. It would be great if you'd do that; you're closer to them than we are, and ever since they released Gary's name, everyone who ever knew him is calling the tip line."

"No problem. I'll do it this morning."

"Thanks. We discovered last night that Gary flew to Pittsburgh. It was a short flight and had already landed by the time we got the information. The FBI and the Pittsburgh police are on the case."

"So now we just wait?"

"I guess. Captain Alexander asked us to organize our files and prepare to take on another case, but the tip line has buried us."

"Who is the FBI Special Agent in charge?" I asked.

"It's our old buddy, MacKenzie, from the Karpovski case."

"Are you kidding?" A year ago, Special Agent MacKenzie's team was staking out a mob hitman, Boris Karpovski, in Brooklyn—and so was I. Karpovski eluded the Feebs, but I ended up shooting him on the street a few blocks from his apartment. The FBI tends not to like it when you show them up, but that wasn't my intent—Karpovski shot at me first.

"What are the odds of that?"

"I have no Idea. I'm sure he'll be thrilled that you're involved," Willy laughed.

"All right, I'll let you know if anything comes up while speaking with the families."

"Okay. Bye, Dan."

AFTER I TOLD each family we believed this was our guy, they all appreciated my call. Doug Morgan offered me a bonus, which I declined. I saved the call to Joan Patterson for last because of Amy's relationship with Gary. I feared that she might feel some guilt for knowing him.

"Hello, Joan. How are you doing this morning?"

"Was Amy really killed by her boyfriend?" Her voice cracked.

"It looks that way, but we don't know for sure."

"He seemed like such a nice young man." The sadness and regret in her voice were apparent.

"There's a reason why husbands and boyfriends are always the prime suspects."

"I thought I'd feel better when the killer was caught, but now I feel worse."

"That's understandable, Joan, but there was no way for you to know. Is there anything I can do for you?"

"I don't think so, but thanks for asking."

We chatted for another few minutes, and she asked how we found out it was Gary. I tried to comfort her with my answers without giving away too much inside information. After finally saying goodbye, I felt terrible for her.

I SAT FOR a while, reliving all that had occurred, and assumed the case was a wrap, at least for me. I then called my partner to see if he needed help with the collector cars.

"There's still a backlog, so if you're looking for something to do, you're welcome to take some off my hands," Jim said.

"Good. I'll come in after lunch and take on a few."

"I'm looking forward to hearing the latest on the nurse murders."

"I'll fill you in; a lot went down this week."

WHILE SORTING THROUGH the car assignments that afternoon, I told Jim about everything that had happened since we last spoke. He was fascinated by the twists and turns and wanted to hear more about the whole asphyxiation scene. I told him what I knew about the case and what I'd learned about the kink. While Jim was taking it all in, he tipped his head and cracked his neck. Having observed this habit of his more frequently, I wondered if he had injured himself and asked, "Did you hurt your neck?"

"I don't know. It's a little stiff, but cracking it seems to help."

"Have you seen a doctor?"

"Nah. It's not that bad yet."

I managed to complete two abstracts of title before the end of the day, and could see there were plenty more assignments to keep us busy.

I SPENT THE next few days at the office while watching the morning and evening news for anything about Gary Leonard. There were no reports of his whereabouts. On Wednesday, Willy called.

"How ya doin', Dan?"

"Good, and you?"

"I have no complaints. I thought you might like to hear what the forensics team found in Mahopac."

"Absolutely."

"They were able to confirm DNA matches for all five murdered nurses. The only one who was not in that house was Olivia Wilder. They said that saddle-like machine was a treasure trove of DNA."

"I can imagine it was. Did they test for Ariana Alonzo?"

"I'm not sure. I'll follow up on that."

"Well, it's been less than a week since she was reported missing."

"I don't have much else to report. Bella and I have been assigned to an internet fraud case, and that's been keeping us busy. I did hear from Agent MacKenzie—they've found no trace of Gary in Pittsburgh except for some clerks at the bus station who said they thought they recognized him from pictures."

"Thought?"

"Yeah, that's about it. We still have his phone, so there's no way to trace it, but MacKenzie hopes he uses a credit card somewhere. They're ready to pounce whenever he does."

"Does MacKenzie think he's still in the country?"

"He told me that Gary did not have a passport; nevertheless, customs and immigration are on the lookout, and he hasn't rung any bells with them yet."

"I was thinking about Jenifer, the girl we found in Mahopac."

"What about her?"

"How do you think she got hooked up with Gary? Could she have contacted him through the website?"

"That's a good question. The only thing we know about her is that she lives in Mahopac. Let me check with Bella and see what she says."

"Good. I'm curious."

"I'll let you know."

"Thanks, Willy."

A FEW MINUTES later, I got a call from Elsa Nordstrom. "I heard there was a sex room in the lake house. Can you confirm that?"

"Yes. It was more of a bondage room, actually."

"What was in there?"

"Besides the ropes used to tie up the girl, there was a rack with various bondage devices and a Sybian."

"You mean one of those orgasm machines that you sit on?"

"Yes. With a leather collar hanging over it, chained to the ceiling."

"How does this relate to the nurses?"

"It doesn't."

"What do you mean?"

"Look, I can't tell you everything we've learned; the police don't want that information out there. But maybe I can help you: What if the cases of the murdered young women were more about sex than about being nurses?"

"Tell me more."

"I can't. As of now, it can be assumed that you put it together on your own from what you heard was found in the lake house. A sharp reporter like yourself should be able to figure it out from there."

"Thanks, Dan. I owe you one!"

"Good luck, Elsa."

When I returned to Mia's, she was busy in her library. I opened the case book and thumbed through it, adding to my list of things we didn't know. Some of the young women had no previous connection to Amy or the other nurses, and I wondered if they had connected through the website or some other way. Those questions ran through my head as I went to sleep that night.

THEY WERE STILL bugging me when I awoke. While sipping my first coffee of the day, I heard from Willy.

"Good morning, Dan. Bella and I were just discussing your thoughts on Jenifer. She's planning on going up to see her later today."

"Great. I was also thinking about the others with no link to Amy, particularly Sierra Swan and Melinda Bernardi. Do you suppose you can obtain their internet and credit card records to see if they were ever on the BDSM website?"

"Probably. Now that we have a suspect, I have an excuse to revisit the families for evidence against him. I think they'll cooperate."

"Good. Let me know if you need any help going through the documents."

"I will. By the way, we've been following up with some of the tips that came in. Bella took a call from a young woman who saw the Mahopac lake house on the news. She claims she was there with Amy Patterson in August."

"Yeah? Does she sound legit?"

"Bella thinks so. She's asking Captain Alexander as we speak if he'll grant us the time to interview her. If he says yes, do you want to be in on it?"

"Definitely!"

"Good. I'll get back to you if we can set something up."

"Okay, Willy."

Within half an hour, Willy called and said, "Captain Alexander asked if you'd be willing to interview her."

"Sure. Give me her contact info, and I'll call her."

"Thanks, I'll text it right over."

"Okay, I'll let you know how I make out."

AFTER RECEIVING JENNA Martin's contact info, I made the call. She answered on the first ring, and after introducing myself, I said, "Detectives Grant and Fratelli have asked me to speak with you about the lake house in Mahopac. I can come to you if that's easier."

"You can come to my apartment, so long as you're not driving a cop car."

"No, I drive an old Jeep Cherokee."

"Good. I'll be home all afternoon."

She gave me her address, and we agreed to meet at 2:00.

After grabbing a quick lunch, I took Route 684 to Mount Kisco. My GPS app led me to a three-story, modern, wood-frame apartment building overlooking a pond. Her unit was on the second floor.

When she answered the door, the first thing out of her mouth was, "You have to promise my name won't get out in the media."

"Anything we discuss today will be strictly confidential, Ms. Martin."

"Good. Please come in."

Jenna was white, plump, thirty-ish, and appeared nervous; not unusual for someone making a statement to the police. After explaining my status as a retired detective assisting with the case, she seemed less anxious.

She gestured for me to sit on the sofa while she sat across from me in an upholstered chair. While her place had some feminine touches, I could tell it was furnished on a lean budget.

I said, "So, you said you recognized the lake house on the news?"

"That's right. Amy Patterson took me there in August."

"And how did you know Amy?"

"She and I have been occasional lovers for a few years."

"Go on, please."

"We're both bisexual, or I mean, we were. I was horrified when I heard she was one of the murdered nurses."

"What was the occasion for her to bring you to the house?"

"Well, we always kept our affair a secret. We didn't want anyone to know we were bi. You can see why I don't want this to get out—I have a boyfriend."

"I do. So, why the lake house?" I asked.

"She wanted me to see the room she had set up and try the Sybian."

"Did you have relations in the room with her?"

"I did."

"All right, I don't need details. Did you ever meet the owner of the house, Gary Leonard?"

"Yes. We had a threesome on my second visit."

"How many times were you there?"

"Just twice. They were into all this bondage shit, choking, and breath play. When Amy tried to choke me, I ended it quick!"

"Did you know any of the other nurses?"

"No. I'm not a nurse."

"Amy had regular Friday night get-togethers at a bar in White Plains. Did you ever attend?"

"No. She invited me once, but it sounded like it was all nurses."

"How did you meet?"

"I sold her a car; we became attracted to each other, and met later for a drink."

"Is that your line of work?"

"Yes, I work at a dealership. I'd rather not say which one."

"That's okay; I don't need to know. Tell me more about the 'bondage shit,'" I urged, making quotation marks in the air.

"Well, they had handcuffs attached to a metal rack and ropes tied to the bed posts. There was also a choking collar chained to the ceiling. While I can get off being restrained and using toys, they were a bit extreme."

"Is there anything else that might help us?"

"Not that I can think of."

"Okay. Thanks for speaking with me today, and don't worry; this will remain between us."

"Thank you for that. I hope you nail that creep," Jenna said as she walked me out.

While driving back, it felt like a waste to make the trip all the way up there for such a short conversation. However, talking to her in person gave me a sense of her honesty, and I believed every word she said. I called Willy.

"What do you think?"

"She sounded very credible to me, but there's not much in her story to use against Gary."

"Yeah, she sounded credible on the phone. Otherwise, we wouldn't have asked you to meet her."

"Everything she said confirms the lake house scenario."

"I don't see a need to follow up unless there's a court trial someday. She could corroborate other testimony."

"Yup, anything else?" I asked.

"That's it. I'll let you know if forensics comes up with anything new."

"Okay, bud. Enjoy your weekend."

WHEN I RETURNED to Mia's, she was washing a whole duckling in the kitchen sink. She turned her head for me to kiss her, then returned to her task.

"How about making martinis this evening, love?"

"Sure. It doesn't look like you're ready, though."

"I'll just be another few minutes."

While I rounded up the ingredients, I watched as she frenched the duck. Whenever I ate a duck or chicken prepared this way, I always wondered how it was done. After cutting the bird in half, she carefully used a boning knife to cut the meat from the bones, leaving the wing, lower leg, and skin intact. It was obvious she had done this before, as there seemed to be a well-trained method to the madness.

A few minutes later, she said, *"Voila!"* and laid the two halves on a baking pan, skin side up, and washed her hands. When they were dry, I handed her a martini.

"Thank you, love."

"Where did you learn how to do that? It seems impossible."

"At a cooking school in France. It's not that difficult once you know how."

"And you didn't even cut yourself!"

"That's the goal," Mia laughed as we moved to the kitchen table with our drinks.

"So, how was your day?"

"Great, I'm pumped because we just signed a contract to design dresses for a famous Italian fashion house. This could be the only work we need, and we may have to hire some help."

"I suppose you'll be going to Milan all the time now?"

"At least a few times—you'll go with me, won't you?"

"I'd like that—I've never been to Italy."

"You'll love it. Maybe we can take a few extra days and see some sites."

"I'm up for it."

"Once I put this duckling in the oven, I'm going to bathe. Then we can sit in the other room and celebrate."

"Shall I chill some champagne?"

"Sure. I have plans for you later," she said as she leaned closer and kissed me.

"Hey, I'm fifty-six now, you know," I smiled.

"Don't give me that, Dan Burnett. I know your capabilities!"

I put a bottle of Champagne in the fridge while she slid the foil-covered duck into the oven and disappeared up the stairs. While she was bathing, I wondered what I had ever done to deserve a woman like her. She was wealthy, talented, a fabulous cook, and the sexiest woman alive.

A short while later, Mia returned, wearing a loose-fitting, silky outfit that resembled pajamas. When I commented on it, she referred to it as loungewear. While seated in our happy place, she shared more about her Italian connection as we sipped champagne.

When we sat down to dinner, the golden-brown duck halves were topped with glazed apricots and accompanied by sticky black rice. The flavor matched the dish's beauty, as the skin was crisp and the meat tender. With the prior deboning, I could just slice off a piece.

"Just amazing, sweetheart!"

"I'm glad you like it."

"I love it!"

Savoring each bite, I remained silent until it was gone. Afterward, I went upstairs to shower, and when I came out, Mia was waiting for me in bed, with the lights dimmed, wearing nothing.

CHAPTER 19

On Monday morning, Willy called. "How was your weekend, Dan?"

"Wonderful."

"That's good to hear. Okay, two things: first, forensics found no evidence of Ariana Alonzo being in the lake house, and second, Bella spoke with Jenifer on Saturday—let me put her on."

A moment later, I heard, "Hi, Dan."

"Hey, Bella."

"So, at first, Jenifer wouldn't tell me a thing. But after a while, when I convinced her that anything she told me would remain private and that we needed the information to prevent Gary from harming other women, she told me about contacting him through the website."

"Good for you, Bella."

"She said she had never done anything like that before, but she had watched some porn with breath play scenes and was curious. After visiting the website, her curiosity got the best of her, and she set up a meeting with Gary, who picked her up in town and took her to the lake house. She said she was nervous, but he was nice to her, and she initially enjoyed herself. She told me that after a while, he became rough and choked her until she passed out. When she woke up, it was dark, and she was tied to the bed the way we found her with the ball gag in her mouth so she couldn't scream."

"Is that it?"

"Not quite. She said that just after daylight, he returned to the room and had sex with her while tied up. He didn't use a condom and choked her again as he finished. They should have gotten a good DNA sample with the rape kit."

"I'm glad you went with her to the hospital. How is she coping?"

"Not well. She clutched and twisted a handkerchief the whole time I was with her, and said she felt ashamed and dirty. Besides that, she's worried she could be pregnant or have a disease."

"Has she talked to a shrink yet?"

"I don't think so. I should have asked."

"I'll text you the contact info for someone who would be perfect. My daughter saw her after she was kidnapped."

"Great. I'll make sure Jenifer gets it. Here's Willy."

When Willy returned to the line, he told me he had called Sierra and Melinda's parents and had appointments later in the day to pick up their computers, phones, and credit card statements.

"Would you like some help going through it all tomorrow?" I asked.

"Yeah, that would be great."

"Okay. I'll be there tomorrow around 9:00."

"See you then, Dan."

After texting Lisa Robbins' contact information to Bella, I headed to the office to help Jim with the collector cars. Although the work was monotonous, it paid the bills. We could always hope for something interesting, like last year's antique collector car case or the stolen Aston Martin from a couple of months ago.

The next day, I arrived at the 50th Precinct as promised. After pouring ourselves coffee, we went to work. Bella said she would handle the computer history because she had the software. Willy searched through the phones while I did the credit card statements. Willy and I were done by lunchtime, but Bella was still entering data. While she finished up, Willy and I went next door to bring back lunch. We all ordered the same thing as last time, and when I asked if they ever got tired of salad and chicken, they lifted their shirts and showed me their abs. No further explanation was required.

When we were done eating, we compared our findings. From Willy's work with the phones, he discovered that Sierra and Amy had called each other. Until then, we had been going by my list of friends, which Sierra's parents and fiancé had supplied. I found that Melinda had paid for a BDSM website mailbox from the credit card records, and Bella confirmed that they both had done searches for erotic asphyxiation on the website.

The three of us contemplated all that for a few minutes before Bella said, "Does it really matter if they were nurses or not?"

Willy replied, "Well, if we put any weight on Jenna Martin's story, I guess not. That was just one way for them to connect. At the end of the day, they were all into breath play as a sexual kink. But what we don't know is who killed whom. We're fairly certain that Amy is responsible for Olivia Wilder's death in June. She may also be responsible for the deaths of Laura Kelly and Sierra Swan."

Bella asked, "Do we think Amy choked herself to death by hanging like the website pictures, or did Gary do it?"

"There's no way to know, but we know they were all at Gary's lake house and went for a ride on the Sybian. Only Gary could be responsible for Melinda's death because Amy was already gone by then," Willy stated.

"And how about Ariana Alonzo?" I asked.

"The forensics team claims they don't have a sample of her DNA," Willy explained.

"What's up with that?"

"I'm told the New Rochelle and Larchmont Police are handling the case together. Because she wasn't a nurse, they're not lumping her in with the others."

"Well, it sounds like we've taken it about as far as we can," I said.

"Yeah, the only question remaining is whether it was Amy or Gary who choked them to death," Bella concluded.

"So, we're confident that Amy and Gary acted as a couple?"

"At least with some of them."

"Can we release this to the public?" I asked.

"Let's share this with the Captain. We'll see what he wants to do with it."

Willy said, "I'll buzz him. Do you want to be in on this, Dan?"

"Sure."

With that, Willy called Captain Alexander. After a few words, Willy said, "He'll meet us in the conference room."

The three of us went down the hall, took a seat, and the Captain joined us a moment later. "So, you think you guys have this all wrapped up?"

Willy and Bella went through the whole thing, explaining the facts that led to our theory. Captain Alexander nodded at each conclusion. When they were done and had stated that the only question was which one of them actually did the strangulations, Captain Alexander said, "Good job, people. It all works for me. Now write it up so I can share it with the Chief."

He rose from his seat and shook our hands before returning to his office. Knowing the task of putting it all in writing would take Willy and Bella the rest of the afternoon, we high-fived before I left them to it.

While driving back to Mamaroneck, I pondered the big question: *Where was Gary Leonard?* I assumed the FBI would find him, and felt content knowing we'd put it all together. It was now just a matter of bringing him to trial. He only needed to be proven guilty of one murder, and there was plenty of evidence to convict him of Melinda's death. There would also be rape and kidnapping charges for Jenifer Jordan. I was confident that he would spend the rest of his life in prison.

I ARRIVED AT Mia's before she did and saw her text that she was on the train, heading home. I went upstairs to shower and was on my way back down as she pulled into the driveway. In the kitchen, I shook up a batch of Cosmos, poured two, and handed her the pale pink elixir when she had set down her things.

After a quick kiss, she said, "Thanks, love. Let's take these to our happy place—I have some good news." She sat on her legs beside me and continued. "I need to be in Milan next week, and I'd like you to go with me. Do you have a valid passport?"

"I'll have to check. The last time I used it was a few years ago while escorting a felon from Canada."

"We're thinking of leaving Sunday night, so I'll have a day to adjust to the time zone before meetings on Tuesday and Wednesday."

"We?"

"I'm sorry, Sandy and I. She'll be flying right back, but I thought we could stay a few extra days and go to Rome."

I wasn't sure I wanted to be a third wheel on a business trip to Italy, especially when I had never met Sandy. But I said, "I'll go to the boat tomorrow and dig out my passport."

"Okay, let me know as soon as you can so we can make flight reservations."

I nodded and took another sip while Mia explained what prompted the Milan trip. When she asked about my day, I told her about the conclusion that Willy, Bella, and I had reached. She wanted all the details, so I filled her in. When finished with the story, she was amazed that there were that many women who wanted to be choked during sex. She was also surprised that a woman did some of the killing.

After finishing our drinks, we returned to the kitchen, where I watched the news while Mia prepared dinner. The top stories were still the teenage girl in Mahopac, the search for the nurse killer, and whether the crimes were related.

Mia announced that dinner was ready, and we sat down to plates of chicken Francese with a lemon, white wine, and butter sauce served with linguine. It was her first time serving that dish to me, furthering my amazement at her culinary repertoire.

"This is fantastic, Mia. And you whipped this up so quickly!"

"Yeah, this is an easy one. I'm glad you like it."

I just smiled, realizing again how fortunate I was.

THE FOLLOWING DAY, while Mia was working from home, I drove to the marina in search of my passport. By the time I arrived, I realized I had been hoping the passport had expired. Analyzing my feelings a bit more, it wasn't just the third wheel thing—I felt uncomfortable with Mia paying my way. I'm sure she would just call it a business expense, but I guess I'm too old school to feel good about that.

From the beginning of our relationship, we were both aware of how our income disparity could be an issue, and she'd always been willing to pick up a tab or pitch in to share an expense without emasculating me. So long as I didn't think like a Neanderthal, it was working out. Yet, deep down, I was still uncomfortable with it.

ARRIVING AT THE marina, I located a ladder and worked my way between the tightly packed boats. Most of them, including *Privateer*, were covered in white shrink wrap. After placing the ladder, I climbed up, unzipped the door in the shrink wrap, and entered a strange world under the white plastic tent. Instead of nothing but sky above me, having plastic a foot or two over my head seemed eerie. Once inside, I rummaged through the drawer containing my essential papers and found the passport. It had expired two years ago.

I called Mia. "I'm sorry, sweetheart, but my passport expired in 2022."

"Oh, that's too bad. We would have had so much fun!"

"I'll work on renewing it right away."

"That can take a while."

"You're probably right. I'll see if they have an expedited option."

"Okay. Bye, love."

THAT AFTERNOON, DOUG MORGAN called. "Hi, Dan. Do you have a minute?"

"Sure," I replied, welcoming the break from searching through titles.

"Can you explain why there's been no arrest yet?"

"Well, the guy is on the run. He was tracked to Pittsburgh last week, and the FBI is searching for him. I'm sure they'll find him eventually."

"Eventually? That sounds pretty vague."

"I'm sorry, I guess it does."

"Do you think you can do better than the FBI?"

"Probably not, considering all the resources they have."

"I'm still willing to renew our contract. Think about it."

"I appreciate that, Doug. Let's see how this progresses."

"Okay. Thanks, Dan."

Jim overheard my side of the conversation and asked, "What was that all about?"

"That was one of the nurses' fathers. You may recall that $2000 retainer I took a while ago—he wants to rehire me."

"And he thinks you can do what the Feebs can't?"

"I guess. He must have an unrealistic opinion of my skills," I chortled.

"You know, your track record would lead one to believe that." Jim tipped his head to the right and cracked his neck.

I returned to my tasks and didn't give Gary more thought for the rest of the day. But while driving to Mia's, I wondered if anyone was looking for friends or family that he may have run to. I called Willy.

"Hey, Dan. What's up?"

"Listen, I'm sorry if I'm being a pain in the ass with all these calls."

"Not a problem. What's on your mind today?"

"I presume the Feebs are looking at friends Gary might have gone to?"

"I'm sure that's the first place they'd look."

"Did they ever search his house?"

"Not under our warrant, or we would have accompanied them."

"What do you think about searching his house again? I mean, I'm sure you were looking for evidence of the killings the first time there, but did you look for letters, notes, address books, etc.?"

"We would have taken an address book if there was one, but there wasn't. I get where you're coming from, though."

"Can you get back in?" I asked.

"The warrant is good for thirty days. Do you want to go?"

"Sure, anytime."

"Let me speak to the Captain, and I'll let you know."

"Okay, Willy. Talk to you later."

Ten minutes later, he texted:

We're on for tomorrow at 9 a.m. See you in Elmsford.

I ARRIVED EARLY the following morning and wandered around Gary's yard, not looking for anything specific, just poking around. When Willy and Bella arrived, he told me he'd notified the Elmsford police that we'd be going in that morning. He also asked Agent MacKenzie if they had searched the house and was told they had, but found nothing useful.

There was now a police lock on the door that Willy unlocked using a combination, and we stepped inside. Everything was in disarray, either from Gary leaving in a hurry or the Feebs trashing the place. Each of us took a room and began a thorough search. We examined every piece of paper in the house, hoping to find any indication of a friend or relative.

Bella was searching a bedroom when she found a letter tucked in a book. It was written on perfumed pink paper in a female hand and signed: Love, Maria. The matching envelope did not have a return address, but the postal stamp was from Columbus, Ohio, dated December 20, 2022.

I searched a desk loaded with bills and statements. Many were in unopened envelopes and scattered about. Either Gary was extremely unorganized, or the Feebs made a mess of them. I found bank and credit card statements from Bank of America, and among them were bank statements from Wells Fargo Bank for an account in Columbus, Ohio. It was a joint account with Maria Leonard. I took it to the room where Bella was searching and showed it to her.

"Could this be a sister?" I asked.

"The letter I found was not from a sister. Unless they were incestuous."

"Could he have been previously married?"

"There's a wrinkle for you," she chuckled.

We spent the rest of the morning rummaging through the attic and basement, but found little else of interest. We looked for anything taped to the bottom of drawers or the back of furniture. Willy went through his pickup and garage. I even went through the freezer, having previously found evidence there during a search years ago. Nothing.

Before leaving, I called Joan Patterson. "Hi, Joan, Dan Burnett again. Sorry to bother you."

"You're never a bother, Dan. What's up?"

"Do you recall Gary ever being gone for an extended period?"

"Just when he went to college, I remember his sweatshirts—he went to Ohio State."

"Did he have a sister?"

"No brothers or sisters—I would have known if he did."

"Thanks, Joan. Those are the only questions I have."

"Bye, Dan."

Willy and Bella were listening to my side of the call. I said, "Gary went to Ohio State; I think that's in Columbus."

"It is," Bella stated.

"And he didn't have any siblings," I added.

Willy said, "So, we'll go with a wife?"

"Or kissing cousins," I quipped.

"We should share this with MacKenzie," Willy said.

"Let's bounce this off the Captain and see what he wants us to do with it," Bella suggested.

With that, they returned to their precinct while I drove to the office in Scarsdale. There were plenty more abstracts of title to be done.

Willy called after lunch to tell me he had shared the info with Agent MacKenzie and that Captain Alexander said we had no choice; it was from out of state.

While driving to Mia's at the end of the day, I realized she would be flying to Europe in just two days. I stopped at a florist and bought a dozen yellow roses, writing on a card how much I would miss her.

When I presented them to her, she said, "They're beautiful!" She read the card, smiled, and went up on her toes, kissing me. The kiss lingered, and with her hands firmly cupping my behind, Mia pulled me close, setting the tone for the weekend.

We thoroughly enjoyed our weekend together, even with her running around, packing, and repacking on Sunday. When I dropped her off late in the day at JFK, she gave me a kiss to remember before exiting the car. My eyes followed as Mia walked through the revolving door, and I knew I would miss her.

After battling traffic for the next hour, I was hungry by the time I reached the house. When I opened the fridge in search of something to eat, I saw three dinners prepared for me in foil containers, each with cooking instructions attached. There were two more in the freezer. *What did I ever do...*

CHAPTER 20

Willy called me Monday morning while I was drinking coffee and watching TV.

"I just got off the phone with MacKenzie," he began. "While they knew he attended Ohio State, they knew nothing about a wife. They spent the weekend trying to track her down and found her in a drug rehab. From what Mackenzie told me, she's been in and out of rehab, mostly in, over the last few years. He said they couldn't find any record of a divorce."

"Did they speak with her?"

"Not yet. The rehab is protective of their patients, but he thought they could see her this week after speaking with an administrator."

"No sign of Gary Leonard?"

"None. The rehab told them Maria had no recent visitors."

"He could still be in Columbus, but just hasn't seen his wife."

"True. But until he uses a credit card, goes to a bank, or someone makes him from a wanted poster, he's in the wind."

"Do you think they put a watch on the Wells Fargo account?"

"Dan, this is the FBI we're talking about—they're not idiots. I'm sure they're watching the account."

Admonished, I challenged, "I wonder. They didn't know about the wife until you told them!"

"You got me there."

"Okay, Willy. Thanks for the call."

My only mission for the day was to renew my passport. By selecting the expedited delivery, they claimed I would have it in a few weeks. That sounded optimistic, but we'd see. After doing that online, I remembered promising to have a beer with Matt Frost a few weeks ago. I texted him, hoping he'd meet me somewhere after his shift. He texted back: Murph's, 5:00. As always, Frosty was efficient with his words.

Later that afternoon, I strolled into Murph's a few minutes after five. Frosty was already at the bar, enjoying a pint of Guinness—his beverage of choice. As I sat beside him, Murph set a cold bottle of Heineken in front of me with just a nod. Murph had run this bar for at least as long as I'd been a cop, and hadn't changed a thing in over thirty years. The interior was dominated by dark wood, dim lighting, and worn vinyl upholstery. On the walls hung vintage neon beer signs, some of the brands I'd never heard of.

When Frosty and I moved to our usual seats at a booth across from the bar, he said, "So the word is, you're working with Willy Grant on the nurse cases."

"I am. We think the perp is the same guy who tied up the girl in Mahopac."

"I saw the BOLOs; he's on the run?"

"Yeah. Last we heard, he was in Pittsburgh, but there's been no sign of him since."

"I hope they find him soon. Since they released his name, people have been calling the precinct every day with tips on his whereabouts.

One woman called to report a creepy guy in the waiting room at a doctor's office. She thought he was stalking the nurses."

"I can imagine. What else have you been working on?"

"Some kids are holding up bodegas with handguns and demanding the money in the registers. It's nickel-and-dime stuff—not many people use cash anymore."

"Even in the Bronx?"

"Yeah, the banks will give a debit card to anyone nowadays."

We each ordered a second beer while Frosty caught me up with everything going on at the precinct before heading home for dinner with his family. On previous occasions, I would usually eat at Murph's once Frosty left. But I'd been thinking all day about the braised pork chops with shallots and tomatoes awaiting me in Mia's refrigerator.

THE FOLLOWING DAY, I saw Elsa on the morning news. This time, she was standing before a magnificent suburban home in Larchmont. The house was huge and beautifully landscaped, with a stone facade around the front door and third-floor window dormers. Elsa told us, "When the owners returned home from an overseas trip, they immediately knew something terrible had occurred because of an overwhelming smell. They found the body of Ariana Alonzo in their king-sized bed, who was the agent handling the sale of their home."

The camera zoomed in on a for-sale sign along the street with Ariana's picture. Over the next several minutes, we saw a forensics team working on the property.

I found out later from Willy that the coroner had determined the cause of death was strangulation, and there was DNA evidence of sexual activity on the body that would identify the killer. I thought of Miguel and how his worst fears had come to be. He would now be raising an infant son on his own.

Later that afternoon, Elsa was again on TV interviewing Ariana's coworkers at the real estate office. While most of them refused to speak with her, one said she was shocked to learn what happened to Ariana. She went on to say how the biggest fear among female agents was being attacked in a vacant home.

When the station went to commercial, they played a teaser for a special half-hour investigative report called "Breath Play," to be aired that evening with Elsa Nordstrom. In the tease, she claimed this was a dangerous new sex game, and it would immediately follow the network's evening news. I smiled, happy to hear that she had put it together, or was at least on the right track with her investigation.

During the local evening news, the station replayed the coverage from earlier in the day and showed a live interview with the Larchmont Chief of Police. There was nothing new to report except that the forensics team was working on a DNA match, and he hoped to have the results soon. As the story wrapped up, we were told to stay tuned after the national news for a special report from Elsa Nordstrom.

I, of course, stayed tuned. Her special opened with scenes from an emergency room, as someone was wheeled in on a gurney. Due to an oxygen mask and hoses, their gender wasn't apparent. Elsa's voice spoke over the footage, explaining that this was just the latest case of someone nearly being choked to death while playing a sex game called "breath play."

The next scene showed her speaking with a doctor about the cases he'd seen recently, and how some had never made it to the hospital—they'd gone to the morgue instead. Elsa played up the drama pretty well. In the next scene, she was speaking with a sex therapist who explained why this practice had become widespread. Simply put, it increased the pleasure from orgasm. The therapist spoke further about how and why it had this effect physically, before warning about the dangers involved.

After a commercial break, Elsa showed charts and graphs of how the practice was growing nationally and how many people were dying. The charts showed there were between three hundred and a thousand deaths in the United States over the past year; the number varied widely because so many were assumed to be suicides. The charts also showed that up to half a million deaths had occurred worldwide from erotic asphyxiation. As her report wound down, I wondered if she planned to link the story to the murdered nurses. She never did.

It wasn't until the following day that Ariana Alonzo's killer was identified through DNA as Gary Leonard. A few hours after learning that on the news, Willy called.

"I assume you've seen the news this morning?"

"I have. Gary has been one busy boy!"

"That he has. How about Elsa Nordstrom's report last night?"

"I saw that, too."

"I'm guessing she went off on that tangent from what was found in Mahopac."

"Most likely," I agreed.

"Listen, MacKenzie called to tell me they spoke to Maria Leonard. She told them she hadn't heard from Gary in two years and confirmed they were still legally married, as far as she knew."

"How coherent was she?"

"He said she had been clean for two months and seemed fine. He also said she had a Spanish accent."

"Interesting. I guess Maria could be a Spanish name."

"Yeah, for sure. That's my news for today."

"Thanks. Bye, Willy."

WHEN I PICKED up Mia at the airport on Friday afternoon, watching her walk toward me sent a rush of joy throughout my body. I hopped out of the car, opened the rear hatch, tossed in her luggage, and hugged her. It wasn't until the traffic cop broke us up that I released her.

On the way to the house, she told me all about her trip and how excited she and Sandy were to work with this designer. She rambled on for a half-hour about things I knew nothing about, but I nodded as if I understood just to hear her voice, happy to have her near me. When she finally asked about my week, I told her the highlight was the premade dinners she left for me.

Once inside the house, I carried her luggage upstairs, and we showered together. It wasn't long before we were desperately making love, standing in the shower with Mia's legs wrapped around me and her back pinned to the wall.

Later, while enjoying Manhattans in our happy place, she said. "You know, we've been together for a year now and still behave like teenagers. How long can that last?"

"I hope forever!" I exclaimed. "This may be a heavy subject for this moment, but I would marry you in a heartbeat if that's what you wanted."

She looked at me, her eyes moistened, and said, "You're right; that is a heavy subject. Are you sure you want to get into it?"

Suddenly realizing the many ways this could go, I considered it momentarily, then bravely said, "Since I raised it, I suppose it's as good a time as any."

"Don't think I haven't thought about it. When Judy and I were together in Portugal, we discussed it at length. Here's the thing: I love how we are now, like Kurt and Goldie—I'd be afraid it would change us."

"It wouldn't have to."

"That's true. But we've both been down that road before. What benefit would there be to being married? I mean, do we really need a legal document? Neither of us relies on the other financially, and we're too old for children. Would it prove we love each other? Would it keep us together if we no longer wanted to be?"

Looking into each other's eyes, our faces just inches apart, we communicated at the most base level possible. I said softly, "I see you have thought about it. I guess it would just be a vow of commitment."

"Our commitment to each other is something we feel in our hearts. That's enough for me."

"It's your call, sweetheart. Just so that you know how important you are to me."

Holding my head in her hands, she touched her forehead to mine with misty eyes and said. "If that was a proposal, thank you. I'm not saying no; I'm saying why. You must know I love you more than anything in this world."

With nothing more to add, we quietly remained in our happy place, holding each other and kissing occasionally until the sun went down. *I wasn't disappointed—far from it. Mia was right.*

OTHER THAN HER Saturday morning trip to the grocery, we spent a quiet weekend at home, never venturing out and spending most of our time in our happy place. She prepared some fabulous meals, and we made love a few times, relishing our time together. It was good to have her home.

LATE MONDAY MORNING, Willy called. "Agent MacKenzie just informed me that Gary showed up at the rehab over the weekend and took Maria with him. They drained the Wells Fargo account and used his Bank of America debit card to withdraw $9000 this morning. It sounds like they're on the run."

"With that much cash, he won't have to use a credit card for quite some time."

"You've got that right. That's all the info MacKenzie had for me, but he said they would place teams at the airport, bus, and rail stations, and her apartment."

"It seems like the Feebs are always one step behind," I said.

"Yeah, it does."

"You told me she had a Spanish accent. Do they know where she came from?"

"I don't know. He said he'd touch base later—I'll ask him."

"Okay, Willy. I'll let you know if I think of anything else."

I SPENT THE next few minutes thinking about what I would do if I were Gary. I imagined all kinds of scenarios and thought leaving the country would be the goal. But without a passport, it would be difficult, and Customs and Immigration were already on the lookout. I wondered if they could settle in a remote area in the United States and start a new life under the radar with new identities.

Later that afternoon, Willy called again. "I spoke to MacKenzie. Gary and Maria took her car, which already had a BOLO on it. The Feebs also did some research with the Department of Homeland Security—Maria was in the country legally and had a green card. She originally crossed the southern border in Laredo, Texas, eight years ago, seeking asylum, which was granted two years later in 2018. In her paperwork, she claimed to be from Tamaulipas, Mexico, and her reason for seeking asylum was fear of drug cartels that murdered her brother."

"How much faith do you have in that story?"

"I have no idea. It could be one hundred percent true, or maybe she told them what they needed to hear to grant her asylum."

"As I recall, a passport is unnecessary to enter Mexico on foot. How secure is the crossing in Laredo?"

"Not very; a lot of people go back and forth for work. That area of Texas would be nothing if not for immigrant labor. MacKenzie already has a team looking for them on the Texas side."

"So, I guess we just sit back and wait for the FBI to do its thing?"

"Well, I have no jurisdiction outside the state of New York. Unless you think you can do something the Feebs can't?"

"The only thing I can think of is to track down any family Maria may have there."

"I'm sure the FBI is already doing that."

"You're probably right. Who knows, maybe they're just hiding out in Montana," I laughed.

"Could be. Time will tell."

Speaking about passports reminded me that my renewal was due to arrive any day now. When I retrieved the mail, it was in the pile.

While Mia and I were having dinner that evening, she reminded me that this Thursday was Thanksgiving. "We're invited to Judy's unless you want to spend the day with Hannah?"

"I'm sure Hannah's mother will want her at the house, and if we were invited, we would have heard about it by now. I'll check with her and let you know."

While Mia was cleaning up, I called Hannah.

"Hi, Dad. We haven't spoken in a while. How are you and Mia?"

"We're both good, Han. It's so good to hear your voice—I've missed you."

"I've missed you, too."

"How's the job going?"

"Great. I got a raise already."

"Good for you. What are your plans for Thanksgiving?"

"Mom invited Frank, and Ken is with his parents. So I guess it'll be just the three of us. She assumed you'd be spending the day with Mia."

"I'm glad to hear Frank is still in the picture."

"Yup, I see him every few days."

"That's good to hear. Mia and I have been invited to her sister's house, but I wanted to check with you before I said yes."

"Thanks. Maybe we can get together over the weekend."

"I'd like that. I'm sure Mia would like to see you, too."

"I'll call you Friday, then."

"Okay, Han. Love you!"

"Love you, too, Dad!"

I told Mia we were good to go to Judy's.

"Great! How about inviting Hannah over this weekend? I'll cook," she said.

"Lasagna again?"

She laughed, "I'll do something else; she might think that's the only thing I know how to make!"

"I'll leave it to you."

"Oh, look at the moon's reflection on the water. Let's take our wine to the other room," Mia suggested.

"After you."

WE ENJOYED OUR Thanksgiving at Judy's, and I met her college-aged children, Mike and Nicole. Sometimes, at an event like this, meeting someone new over a holiday can be an uncomfortable experience. But they seemed intrigued to meet Aunt Mia's new boyfriend. Mike wanted to hear all about being a detective and asked me questions for an hour.

Between Judy and Mia's cooking, there was more food than four people could possibly eat, so the kids loaded up and brought container after container back to school. I thought they'd have enough food to feed the whole dorm. After they left, the three of us sat around drinking coffee and chatting while I got to know Judy a little better. It was uncanny how she seemed like a slightly older version of Mia. Even her laugh was the same.

HANNAH ARRIVED LATE afternoon on Saturday for dinner. With another hour of sunlight, we bundled up for a beach walk. As always, the seagulls were out and about doing their thing. They seemed to be watching us, hoping we'd drop something edible.

Walking westward, as the setting sun warmed our faces, Hannah asked, "Is this where you found the nurse's body?"

"A little way further up—I'm not sure exactly," I replied.

Pointing, Mia added, "It was just past the driftwood log, which I'm surprised is still there."

We walked as far as the driftwood, sitting, pausing to rest. I remarked, "Who would have thought finding that first body a few months ago would have opened the door to all those murders?"

"Certainly not me," Mia said.

"Is it all over, Dad?"

"Unless there's another body still in the water. The perp is on the run, and he'll never return—except maybe in handcuffs," I told her.

Mia and Hannah hooked my arms and each hugged a shoulder. "Thanks to you, love," Mia said.

Our return trip was upwind and felt colder, causing them to tighten their grip on my arms.

Once back in the house, Mia made tea to warm us. She had put a standing rib roast in the oven before we left for our walk, and by the time we finished our tea, the aroma was wafting through the house. An hour later, we sat in the dining room, the first time it had been used for eating since I had been there. The roast beef was cooked perfectly, and she served it with au jus, horseradish, and pan-roasted root vegetables.

Hannah asked, "Do you always cook like this? It's amazing!"

"Well, we don't have prime rib every night, but I usually make something good—I like to cook," Mia replied.

"She's being modest, Han. Every night is fantastic," I chortled.

"Thank you, love."

Over dinner, Hannah told us about her Thanksgiving, and I asked about her mother and Frank. He was part of the team that rescued Hannah from the kidnappers, and I had immense respect for him.

"They're sort of cute together. While it's weird to see Mom dating, I think they're enjoying themselves—I could see it getting serious."

"I'm happy for them," I said.

A moment later, Hannah exclaimed, "Mia, I'm dying to hear about Milan!"

"Oh, where do I start? Europe is so different from the States. The people aren't as frantic as in New York, and the language and architecture are delightful. I think I'll enjoy working over there."

"Is the food as good as they say?"

"Even better. There's something about the food in Europe that can't be replicated here."

"I'm dying to go," Hannah said.

"Maybe you'd like to come with me sometime."

"Oh my god, I'd love to!"

"I'm still hoping your Dad will come with me."

"Oh," I said. "Did I tell you my new passport came a few days ago?"

"That's good to know," Mia replied.

Hannah's eyes had followed us side-to-side like a tennis match, and she smiled, amused by our banter.

We'd been drinking cabernet with dinner, and after finishing, we took our glasses into the living room. Mia served blueberry pie, leftover from Thanksgiving, while our conversation about Italy continued. A while later, Hannah headed home after hugs and kisses at the door.

By Sunday afternoon, my mind had drifted back to Gary Leonard. Even though I swore not to think about him over the holiday weekend, I wondered how the Feebs were making out. Later that evening, once in bed, Mia made me forget all about him.

CHAPTER 21

On Monday morning, the lead story was from Puerto Vallarta, Mexico. We were told that the previous afternoon, when a cruise ship passenger failed to return from a routine sightseeing stop, the staff searched the stateroom and found the man's wife dead, in the bed, naked. When the shipboard medical staff inspected the body, they found she had been strangled and estimated the time of death to be roughly twenty-four hours earlier. They had not released any names, but I would have bet anything the deceased was Maria Leonard.

Ten minutes later, Willy called. "Have you seen the news yet this morning?"

"I'm just watching it now. Is it Maria Leonard?"

"According to Agent MacKenzie, it is. I'm told this cruise originated in LA for a tour of Mexico's west coast. Puerto Vallarta was the first stop."

"It's terrible to hear he killed his wife, but at least we know where he is."

"Or was. MacKenzie says they're working with the Mexican authorities but have no leads so far."

"I thought the FBI had offices in Mexico?"

"They have some agents there, but primarily work with the local police."

"Wonderful. I'm sure those guys can be bought off for two tamales and a box of bullets."

Laughing, he said, "I'm told they're extremely underpaid down there and consider bribes a perk of the job. If it wasn't for that, there might not be any police at all."

"So the Feebs have to grease some palms for cooperation?"

"I'm sure that's the case."

"How did Gary enter without a passport?"

"United States citizens only need a passport when arriving by airplane."

"Oh yeah, that's right. I appreciate the call."

WHILE THE NETWORK I was watching moved on to other stories, I surfed through other channels for more from Mexico. CNN was covering the story when I tuned in, but after a few minutes, I learned nothing new.

Mia joined me in the kitchen for coffee and noticed what I was watching.

"Strangulation? Is that the nurse killer you've been after?" she asked.

"According to Willy and the FBI, it is."

She sat beside me to hear more. After a few minutes, she asked, "Can the FBI operate in Mexico?"

"Kind of," I answered.

"What does that mean?"

"It means they have agents and offices there, but I think it's more of a diplomatic presence than anything else. They work with the local police for the most part."

"How important is this case to them? The FBI, I mean."

"I don't know. Judging from their efforts here in the States over the last few weeks, I'm not impressed."

Frowning, Mia rose and went to the kitchen to eat a few strawberries, her usual breakfast. Then she disappeared upstairs, I assumed to dress for the day.

LATER THAT MORNING, I received a call from Doug Morgan. "Hey, Dan. I just saw the news report from Mexico. Is that Gary Leonard's doing?"

"We think so."

"It seems the FBI is just running around holding their dicks, waiting for him to turn himself in," he said. "Now he's in a foreign country."

"I get where you're coming from, Doug."

"Listen, if you want to put a few guys together and go there to hunt him down, I'll foot the bill."

"I can appreciate your frustration, but I know nothing about Mexico."

"I'm just saying, the FBI has been jerking off for a month. I think you can do better, even in a foreign country."

"I'm flattered you regard me so highly, Doug. I'll give it some thought."

"Thanks, Dan. I look forward to hearing from you."

I couldn't help but recall the last time I hunted someone down— it ended in a military style raid with shootings and deaths.

A FEW MINUTES later, Sierra Swan's fiancé, Devan Wolfe, called.

I answered, "Hello, Devan. How are you?"

"I'm fine, Dan. I just saw the news about the strangled woman in Mexico. Is that our guy?"

"Yes, we think it's Gary Leonard."

"Can I hire you to go to Mexico and bring him back?"

"This is strange, Devan. I received a call from the father of another nurse a few minutes ago. He asked me the same thing, and I told him I know nothing about Mexico."

"What if we both pay you? Would you do it then?"

"Look, I appreciate the offer, but I'm uncomfortable taking money for something I can't deliver. Let me talk to my partner; I'll call you back if we can figure out a place to start. Is that fair enough?"

"That's fair, Dan. Thanks."

I thought about it for the rest of the morning. Maybe with two people paying us, Jim might be interested. After lunch, I called him. "Do you want to go to Mexico?"

"For work or pleasure?"

"Work. We have two people willing to pay us to find Gary Leonard."

"The same Gary Leonard the Feebs have been chasing around the country for the last month?"

"That's the one, except he's now in Mexico."

"Christ, Dan. What the hell do we know about Mexico?"

"That's what I told them, but they won't take no for an answer."

"How did you leave it with them?" he asked.

"I told them I would speak to my partner to see if we can be effective."

"Effective? We'll be lucky if we don't get lost!"

"I'll stop by and tell you what I know. Maybe you'll have a eureka moment."

WHEN I ARRIVED at the office, Jim had a fresh pot of coffee ready and waiting. I brought the case book with me and reviewed it thoroughly over the next hour. He was undoubtedly familiar with the murdered nurses from our previous discussions and what he had followed on the news. He wanted to hear more about the asphyxiation side of the story. Once I explained everything I knew, he asked about the previous wife, her background, and her murder on the cruise ship.

I told him about Maria's origin and how she arrived in this country. I also shared what I learned about her drug problems and attempts at rehab. Jim was a thorough and methodical detective who could always grasp the big picture.

He weighed it all, cracked his neck, and said, "So the area in Mexico where she was raised and had family is on the eastern border near Laredo, Texas. Gary jumped ship in Puerto Vallarta on the opposite side of the country, hundreds of miles away. What do you make of that?"

I answered, "I think he sprung her from the rehab to help him hide out in Mexico, probably near where she knew people. But then, on the cruise ship, he got carried away during sex and killed her. Without any way of getting rid of the body, he just never returned from the tourist excursion."

"It must have gone down like that—there would be no reason to take her with him if it wasn't to help him hide out. And now he's on the loose with nowhere to go."

"That's my take. What do you think?" I said.

"It's a story that fits what we know. That's about it."

"Where would we start if we were to take this up?"

"Puerto Vallarta, I guess. That's where he was last seen. We should first find out from the cruise line what names they were using. Then we need to research her past and search for family wherever she's from."

"We can probably do both things from right here," I said.

"Let's spend some time on it and see how we do."

"Okay, I'll call Willy to see if he has more information about Maria's past."

"I'll call the cruise line," Jim said, tipping his head and cracking his neck.

With that, we each went to work on the phones.

"Hey, Willy. It's Dan."

"What's up?"

"Do we know what Maria Leonard's maiden name was?"

"I don't. I assume MacKenzie has it."

"What name were they registered under on the cruise ship?"

"I don't know that either. Are you going to pick this back up?"

"We'll see. Right now, I'm figuring out if there's somewhere to start."

"I'll send you MacKenzie's contact info. He'll just love to hear from you!" he laughed.

"Thanks, Willy. I'll keep you posted."

"Good luck!"

While I had been talking with Willy, Jim learned from the cruise line that they had used their real names, but had no knowledge of Gary's current whereabouts—the ship had already moved on. I called Special Agent MacKenzie.

"Mackenzie."

"Hello, this is Dan Burnett calling."

"Yes. Willy Grant told me you were sniffing around the Leonard case."

"I have a client who's paying me for information. Can you tell me Maria's maiden name and where she was from?"

"Her name was Ramirez, and according to her immigration file, she was from Tamaulipas, a state along the eastern border."

"Have you had any luck finding Gary Leonard?"

"I shouldn't be telling you anything, but no, we haven't."

"What kind of personnel do you have down there?"

"The only thing I can say is what we told the media: We're working with local authorities." He didn't sound happy to be speaking with me.

"All right. I get it."

With that short exchange concluded, I relayed the information to Jim.

"Ramirez? That's like Johnson in the United States. There are millions of them," he said.

"Do we have to go down there and search through birth records?" I asked.

"We can probably do it online, but even filtering the name to Maria, there will still be tons of Ramirezes."

"We at least have a place to start. What do you think?"

"I could use a break from the collector cars. Let's get signed agreements from the clients, including a retainer, and give it a shot."

We bumped fists, then I made the calls to Doug Morgan and Devan Wolfe. They were thrilled that we would take on the case, despite my initial doubts about our chances of success. After emailing over our terms of engagement, they both returned them immediately with signatures and permission to bill their credit cards.

Having already determined we would start in Puerto Vallarta, we researched travel arrangements. After getting a feel for available flights, we decided to hold off until Jim spoke with his wife, and I conferred with Mia.

I began tracing Maria's ancestry, hoping to find any living family members. I discovered that Mexico keeps computerized birth records and has an organized database for genealogy searches. I first needed the mother's and father's names, including the mother's maiden name. I found everything from Gary and Maria's marriage license in Columbus, Ohio.

Maria's mother's name was Isabella Cueto, and her father was Carlos Ramirez. The website was organized like a family tree. After entering Maria's name along with her parents', the site requested her place of birth. While I didn't know the town, I entered the state of Tamaulipas, which seemed to be enough. Fortunately, at least in Mexico, Cueto was a less common name than Ramirez. A little while later, I found Maria's birth certificate. She was born in 1996 in Nueva Laredo, bordering Laredo, Texas. The only siblings she had were one brother, Carlos Jr., reported as deceased.

Jim and I briefly questioned our decision to start in Puerto Vallarta, but thought that even if Gary and Maria planned to go to Nueva Laredo, his plans would likely have changed when he killed her. After speaking to our significant others that evening, we booked direct flights from JFK to PVR for the next morning. Jim planned to take an Uber to the airport and pick me up on the way. We confirmed we had the required passports and would be leaving our firearms at home. Mexico was strict about bringing in weapons, with severe penalties. The last thing I did was text Willy with our plans.

CHAPTER 22

The following morning, I kissed Mia goodbye when the Uber arrived. Although our tickets were for economy seats, we were fortunate to have no one in the middle seat, allowing us to speak freely about our mission. We decided to first check in with the local authorities so they would know of our presence. After that, we would canvass the cruise ship terminal with pictures of Gary, hoping someone would have seen him.

Upon arrival, we were surprised by how large and busy the airport was. As we made our way outside to get a cab, we were harassed by people trying to sell us time-shares. Once we had checked into a hotel near the airport to drop off our luggage. Our first impression of Puerto Vallarta was of a busy, touristy city. After a short cab ride to the police station, we asked if anyone had knowledge of the death on the cruise ship and the missing passenger. The station was nothing like the ones in the States. The smell was rank with BO, among other things, and the place was rundown and dirty. A sizeable overhead fan kept the air moving, but it was still the same temperature as outside. Jim pointed out some dried blood spatter on a once-white plaster wall. So far, my preconceived notion of a Mexican Police department was accurate, and I was curious if my vision of the Policia would be, too.

After sitting for a moment, we were greeted by Lieutenant Sanchez. He brought us back to a conference room, where an air conditioner labored in the only window. We told him our reason for being there and gave him one of our pictures of Gary Leonard, along with a fifty-dollar bill. He smiled and made eye contact after pocketing the fifty, then studied the photo carefully and noted the tattoo on Gary's right arm. His English was passable, and he seemed cooperative as he told us he would post the picture and ask his men to be on the lookout. He suggested we exchange contact information, which seemed gracious; I assumed he thought more fifties were available. On our way out, I said, *"Gracias, Lieutenant. Buenas tardes!"*

The cruise ship terminal was only half a mile away, so we walked to experience the feel of the city. While it was warm, it was not as humid as Florida. I'd read tourist information explaining how the Pacific Ocean moderated the temperature in Puerto Vallarta.

As we approached the terminal, the storefronts became more upscale. Once there, Jim and I split up, each with a half dozen pictures. We stopped at tourist counters, food stands, and rental car counters. At that moment, no passengers were coming and going, so many were closed or vacant. Attempting to communicate with anyone proved difficult. A few understood some English, but I understood very little Spanish.

I recalled the phrase *"Le has visto?"* from making the same inquiries in the South Bronx many years before, but I mainly communicated by pointing to the picture. No luck.

Jim led me to a driver at a taxi stand, who said in accented English that he took the man in the picture to the *Zona Roja* a few days before. Even with my limited Spanish, I translated that to Red

Zone. He explained it was where the nudie bars and sex shops were, and offered to take us. We hopped in his cab and asked him to drop us off at the same place he dropped Gary.

Five minutes later, we exited the cab in front of *Club Paradiso*. We glanced around the area and saw a half-dozen similar places, with flashing lights, heavy music pumped out to the sidewalks, and pictures of scantily clad girls. We walked in, sat at the bar, and ordered two light beers, remembering only to drink from a sealed container in Mexico— no local water and no ice.

It was dark inside, and it took a while for our eyes to adjust. The first thing I noticed was how young the dancers appeared to be. Most were teenagers, some—I guessed—as young as twelve or thirteen, with small budding breasts. As the father of a daughter, I found the whole scene gravely disturbing, but as a cop, I'd seen it all before. I wondered if they were the primary breadwinners in their households.

We glanced around at the other patrons, looking for Gary. While we weren't expecting to just bump into him three days after he went missing, we kept our eyes open. We showed the dancing girls our pictures, and so long as we kept handing out dollar bills, they would stay by our side and look. None spoke English, so there was not much in the way of conversation.

They all wanted to take us to a curtained-off room for a private dance. We declined, but other girls came by, having seen us tipping their colleagues—if that was an appropriate term. One of the older girls, maybe nineteen, with large swaying breasts, who knew a little English, said, "I dance for him in private room."

When we asked her when, she told us three days ago, and hinted she knew more about Gary.

She sat on a bar stool between us, told us her name was Mandy, and we bought her a drink. After shooing the other girls away, she managed to rub her breasts on our arms repeatedly while trying to entice us into a private dance. We soon realized her claimed knowledge of Gary was just a ploy to get us to buy her a drink—she knew nothing. I was sure her drink was just juice, and we'd be charged for a drink with top-shelf alcohol.

After leaving *Club Paradiso*, Jim and I wandered the street with our photos, asking anyone we came across if they had seen this man. The music from each place clashed with the others, and we poked our heads in other strip club doors only to be quickly ushered away by bouncers. Further down the street, we encountered a police officer on foot patrol. Along with a badge, he wore a name tag that read "Rivera." After handing him a picture and a twenty-dollar bill, he suggested in perfect English that we look in the park where the homeless live and pointed us in that direction.

We wandered toward the park, continuing to show our pictures and repeating, *"Le has visto?"* Once arriving, we saw a few tents set up, each under a shade tree, but if this were anything like the homeless places around New York, it would start filling up after dark. As the sun went down, we bought street tacos from a food truck and sat on a park bench, hoping Gary would show up. The mixture of competing music blaring from the Red Zone was painful to listen to. Something we assumed the homeless would have to bear all night.

We saw Officer Rivera patrolling the park. When he spotted us, he approached and asked, "Have you had any luck with your manhunt?"

"Not yet," I answered. "Tell me about the homeless here; why this park?"

"As we get into tourist season, we round them up from the beaches and under bridges where the tourists might see them," he said.

"Are there any shelters?"

"Some, but not enough. With this park on the far side of the Zone Roja, the government thinks they're out of sight. Once tourist season is in full swing, many will find jobs and will be able to afford rent."

"Good to hear."

"Yeah. I hope you find your man, *amigos*," he said, then continued his patrol.

At 9:00, with no sign of Gary, we took a taxi back to our hotel. On another day, when less tired, it might have been close enough to walk. Once we reached our separate rooms, I fell asleep with my ears still ringing.

STARTLED, I AWOKE to the sound of gunfire. It sounded like two people shooting at each other. It would be quiet for a minute; then, two guns would fire briefly—three or four shots in succession, each making a different sound. I saw the time was just after four a.m. and texted Jim to make sure he wasn't involved. He returned my text with a thumbs-up emoji.

At 8:00, we met at the restaurant for breakfast, dressed in shorts and polo shirts. After a sip of coffee, I asked, "What do you suppose that gunfire was all about?"

Jim laughed. "It's probably a normal occurrence."

Our waitress greeted us, *"Buenos dias, señores.* What can I get you this morning?"

We both ordered breakfast burritos, and then Jim asked her about the shots we heard overnight. Speaking passable English, she told us she wasn't surprised but didn't live around here, so she knew nothing about it.

I said, "We have a friend visiting Puerto Vallarta, but we don't know where he's staying; we're hoping to run into him. Is there a tourist area everyone goes to where we can hang out?"

"*Sí.* Try the *Malecón*; every tourist goes there."

"Is that walkable?"

"From here, it would take a while. It's past the marina."

"Gracias."

After she left us, Jim said, "We need to get a map and figure out where we are and where everything else is."

"*Sí.*" I smiled.

AFTER BREAKFAST, WE strolled to the front desk and found a rack of maps and information on local tourist attractions. From the map, it appeared we were on the north side of town, and the *Malecón* was on the south side. Maybe we weren't in a central location after all. I spoke to the desk clerk and asked about getting a taxi to the *Malecón*, but they told me they had a free shuttle van leaving in ten minutes. Perfect! While waiting, we scanned the map to understand where things were.

On the shuttle, we passed near the police station and the area we walked the day before. After passing the cruise ship terminal, I asked the driver to let us off, thinking Gary may have walked the area after exiting the ship.

Continuing south on foot, we walked past some older hotels, wondering if Gary was in or had stayed in any of them. We spent the next hour stopping at each hotel, showing our pictures with no luck. We were canvassing, a tiring but necessary part of police work that every rookie cop learns to do. While monotonous, it can be rewarding if you're lucky. Nearing the *Malecón*, the area seemed like the center of attraction, and Jim and I looked at each other, realizing the enormity of our task and how lucky we would have to be to find Gary. Jim tipped his head, cracking his neck.

The *Malecón* was a pedestrian-only walkway along the beach, situated on top of a seawall. We heard it called "the boardwalk," but it was all concrete and stone, not a board to be found. It reminded me of Fort Lauderdale Beach, with hotels and restaurants on one side and the beach on the other, except this one was too rocky for swimming. Nonetheless, people had already claimed the few spots of sand available for tanning.

We were in no hurry and had nothing else to do but keep our eyes peeled. After strolling for a while, we sat on a bench, watching and listening to the breaking waves and observing the people around us. We then resumed walking, looking into each shop or restaurant along the way. Some weren't open this early, but we continued, planning to look again on our way back. When we reached the southern end, it was early afternoon.

We wandered back, even slower if that was possible, looking at every face passing by and peering into every establishment. About halfway, we came across a restaurant with sidewalk tables that served American food. When I saw a chicken salad sandwich on the menu board, we each took a seat.

Jim cracked his neck and said, "This seems impossible. What are the odds of us running into him?"

"I don't know, man. We're getting paid and can expense the lunch. What else do we have to do?"

"I guess you're right. We wouldn't be eating lunch outside in New York in December."

When the waitress came by to take our order, I was surprised that she spoke perfect American English and asked, "How did an American girl end up waiting tables here?"

She looked at me curiously and said, "I was here with my boyfriend and realized I couldn't stand him. I split, and since I had no money, I needed a job. It's as simple as that. What can I get you?"

"Shall we have a beer, Jim?"

"I can't think of a better way to spend the afternoon."

"Two Modelos, please!"

"Coming right up."

When she returned with our beers, I laid a picture on the table and said, "Have you seen this man?"

A look of recognition came over her face. She placed her hand on my seat back and said, "Two days ago, he sat right here, in the same seat you're sitting in!"

Jim and I perked up, looked at each other, and started asking her questions. We learned Gary had been here alone at lunchtime, drank four beers, ate a hamburger, and hit on her the whole time. When she rebuffed him, he left her a shitty tip. I slipped her a twenty before placing our order.

Sipping our beers and watching the passers-by, Jim said, "Well, that's encouraging."

"Maybe we should camp out here."

"It's as good an excuse as any to sit and drink a few beers."

We touched bottles. "Cheers!"

When our waitress delivered our sandwiches, she was all smiles. After ordering two more Modelos, we ate our lunch while enjoying the sun and watching for Gary.

It was after 3:00 when we had finished our third beer. While paying the check, I handed the waitress a fifty, along with my card, and told her there would be another fifty for her if she saw him again and called me.

"Thank you, I'll keep a lookout," she said, her smile beaming.

After leaving, we continued our stroll, with me looking at the people along the beach and Jim watching the bars and restaurants. By the time we reached the end, where we started, we were about out of gas. While we weren't drunk from three beers over two hours, it had made us tired. We spotted a Starbucks on the corner and stopped in for a dose of caffeine, sitting outside to maintain our surveillance while watching the sun creep lower over the ocean.

"So, what do you think?" I asked Jim.

"With the encouragement we got at the restaurant, I think we're making progress."

"I agree, although I feel like the FBI—always a step behind."

"Yeah, we were three days behind at the nudie bar and two days behind on this street. With any luck, tomorrow we'll only be one day behind," Jim laughed.

"What do you want to do now?"

"Maybe go back to our hotel, shower, and take a nap. We can go back out tonight and continue our search."

"Sounds like a plan," I said.

With our coffee cups empty, we rose to leave and dropped them in the trash. As we stepped onto the pedestrian walkway, a man came around the corner, and we collided. It was just a bump, but when I began to apologize, I was looking into the face of Gary Leonard.

I reached out to grab him, but his reactions were quicker than mine, and he took off running back the way he came. Jim realized who it was a moment after I did, and we gave chase.

At the next corner, Gary turned right and headed down the busy sidewalk parallel to the *Malecón*. This street had cars and traffic. Running as hard as we could on irregular cobblestones, we kept up with him, maybe thirty feet behind. He was quick to dodge people on the crowded sidewalk and jumped out into the street to avoid a large crowd. We stayed with him on the street, then back on the sidewalk, evading pedestrians over the next few blocks.

Jim and I were breathing hard but had settled into a maintainable pace. Gary seemed to know where he was going, and the next time there was a break in the traffic, he crossed the road and turned left at the next corner, still sprinting.

Now, heading away from the *Malecón*, Gary was pulling away from us. We kept up our pace, but it was quickly apparent that a couple of guys in their mid-fifties were no match for someone in his mid-twenties. As the distance increased, our only hope was that he would trip on a cobblestone and fall. He never did.

When it was clear we would never catch him, Jim and I stopped, bent over with our hands on our knees, gasping for air. Both red in the face, with our hearts pounding, we took deep breaths until we could stand up straight, wandering around on the sidewalk, gathering ourselves until we could speak.

"Well, we went from three days to two days to zero," I said, still breathing hard.

A minute later, Jim said, "Shall we continue in the direction he was heading to see what's there?"

"Sure."

Back to a stroll, yet still breathing heavily and moist with sweat, we continued east a few blocks and found ourselves in front of a casino. I dug out our map to see exactly where we were. We appeared close to the Red Zone and about the same distance from our hotel as before beginning the chase. Seeing no other obvious place Gary may have gone, we entered the casino.

Glancing around, it was unlike casinos in Las Vegas—much smaller without the grandeur or shops and restaurants. It was just one big room with rows of slot machines lining the perimeter and gaming tables in the center. It was also much too early to be crowded. However, there did appear to be hotel rooms, so I went to the front desk while Jim scanned the casino floor.

"Can you ring Mr. Leonard's room, please?" I asked.

After clicking a few keys, he said, "*Perdón, señor.* We don't have anyone registered by that name."

"Okay. I must have the wrong casino. *Gracias.*"

Jim and I wandered around, looking for Gary while listening to the harmonic din in C major that all slot machines put out. After eyeballing every person in the place, I said, "I guess we lost him."

Jim cracked his neck and said, "Yeah, it looks like it.

"Listen. I'm toast. Let's return to our hotel, and we'll pick this up again tomorrow."

"My thoughts, exactly."

THE DOORMAN HAILED us a cab at the casino entrance. We had planned to shower and nap, but now that we were exhausted, the nap might become a full night's sleep.

I awoke around nine p.m. and texted Jim to ask if he wanted to meet me for dinner. Five minutes later, without a reply, I went down to the restaurant by myself. Once seated, I ordered a ribeye steak, baked potato, salad, and a Diet Coke.

Tired but hungry, I glanced around the hotel's restaurant and noticed a few vacationing couples. Some looked excited about their upcoming stay, while others appeared worn out from a day spent on their feet in the sun. Soon, Jim joined me, asked what I ordered, and told the waitress he'd have the same.

"I hope my text didn't wake you," I said.

"No problem; I'm starving."

"I haven't run like that in five years," I declared.

After cracking his neck, he said, "It's been more like ten for me."

While eating, I asked, "So, we're staying another day or two?"

"For sure. We almost had him by the collar today!"

When the waitress came by with the check, I pulled out a picture and said, *"Le has visto?"*

She studied the picture for a moment and said. "No. *Perdón, señor."*

CHAPTER 23

Jim was drinking coffee when I joined him in the restaurant. "Good morning!"

"How did you sleep?" I asked.

"Like a baby, but my legs are killing me."

"Mine, too. Maybe we should run more often."

"Why?" he laughed.

I smiled, "So where to today?"

"Maybe we should hang out in the area where we chased him yesterday, between the Casino and Starbucks."

"Yeah, we'll start at Starbucks, work our way to the casino, then return to the Red Zone. Since he was heading that way, maybe he hangs out there."

"Could be. We can check out the homeless park again, too."

We had the same breakfast waitress we had the day before, and this time, I pulled out a picture and asked, "Le has visto?"

She studied the picture momentarily and said, "No. *Perdón, señor.* What can I get you?"

After ordering bacon and eggs, Jim said, "If we ran into him on just our second day here, that might be a good omen."

"Do you believe in omens?"

"No. Not really."

Once our breakfast was delivered, we chatted about our prospects. Before finishing, my phone vibrated. It was Lieutenant Sanchez, the cop we spoke to when we arrived in town.

After a *buenos dias*, he said, "One of my men told me a man with a fish tattoo was seen yesterday at a beach bar. It's on a remote cove about ten miles north of here called *Mañana*."

"Is it the cove or the bar that's called *Mañana*?"

"Both, it's on *Mañana* beach."

"Gracias, Lieutenant. We'll check it out."

I filled Jim in on the other side of the conversation, and we both thought it better to follow that lead than our previous plan. Since it was too early to go to the beach bar, we wandered over to the pool area, found some seats in the shade, and called home. While he spoke with Nancy, his wife, I called Mia.

"Dan?"

"Good morning, sweetheart."

"I'll go with good morning, love. But it's afternoon here."

"I'm imagining you're in your library, sketching?"

"Yup. How's it going in Mexico?"

"Well, we haven't captured him yet," I chuckled.

"Really? After a day and a half? You must be losing your touch!"

"We did see him yesterday, though. I physically bumped into him."

"You're kidding."

"No. We literally ran into each other. He took off, and Jim and I chased him through the streets for a mile before he outran us."

"Unbelievable!"

I told her more about our chase, our exhaustion, and today's lead at the beach bar. We spoke about her work for a minute, and then, with nothing left to talk about, we said our goodbyes. Jim's call lasted about the same as mine. I guess after just two days, we hadn't been missed that much. We wandered around the hotel gift shops for another hour, then took a cab to *Mañana* Beach, about a half-hour ride.

Along the way, once out of the city, we saw poverty. Run-down properties and broken-down cars seemed to be everywhere. Occasionally, we'd pass by an elaborate resort on the ocean side with a grand entrance and manicured landscaping—covertly fenced, I'm sure. Then, it was just more poverty, along with an occasional donkey.

We stepped out of the cab into the day's growing heat, happy to be wearing shorts, and wandered through jungle-like foliage on a path marked by wooden signs with "Mañana Beach Bar" carved in them. A few moments later, we saw a tiki bar with a thatched roof set under the trees along an idyllic horseshoe-shaped beach. There were beachgoers already set up for the day, some under umbrellas. They all had deep, dark tans—unlike tourists. This was where the knowledgeable locals came for a day in the sun. After admiring the peaceful setting and the ocean breeze, we noticed someone behind the bar preparing to open.

Jim and I cozied up to the bar near a row of neatly displayed soft drink bottles. We ordered Diet Cokes when the bartender approached us, and after delivering the chilled bottles, we asked if he had worked the previous day.

"Every day, from eleven to sunset, there is no one else," he said in understandable English.

Laying the picture on the bar, with a twenty on top, I said, "*Le has visto?*" pointing to the fish tattoo.

"*Sí*. He was here yesterday," he replied, nodding and pocketing the bill.

"What more can you tell us?"

"He asked where he could rent a boat to go fishing."

"What did you tell him?"

"I told him my brother rents boats at a marina about halfway between here and the city. Pacifico Boat Rentals."

"Can you give me directions?"

"I'll call you a cab; everyone knows it."

"Gracias. We'd appreciate that."

While he made the call, we finished our Cokes and admired the beach, happy to be in the shade. A few minutes later, the bartender announced the cab's arrival. As we headed out, he hollered, "Tell him José sent you!"

TEN MINUTES LATER, we arrived at a tired-looking marina with boats of all sizes in various states of repair. Some were on land, some at docks, and miscellaneous boat parts were scattered everywhere on the ground. Chickens were wandering about, and a dog was sleeping in the shade. The office was a trailer with an air conditioner grinding away in a window. As we approached, the dog lifted his head, and a man stepped out to greet us.

"José said to tell you he sent us."

"Sí, my little brother; I am Julio. Do you want to rent a boat?"

I showed him the picture and asked if he had rented a boat to the man in the photo.

"*Sí*. Yesterday afternoon, he took a boat for a few hours."

"Do you know where he went with it?"

"He said he wanted to explore the area and told me he'd come back to rent it again."

I looked at Jim, wondering if we'd just caught a break. When he cracked his neck again, I realized it had become a habit—he did it while thinking.

"Did he say when he'd return?" I inquired.

"Not exactly, but it sounded like it would be soon."

"How much do you charge for boat rentals?" I asked.

"From thirty to fifty U.S. dollars an hour, plus fuel. I have boats from sixteen to thirty feet, with a four-hour minimum. And that includes fishing gear and a cooler of ice if you want it."

"Can you show us the boats?"

"*Sí.*" Julio turned and headed for the dock as we followed.

"Which boat did he rent?"

"*Aqui,*" he said, pointing to a sixteen-footer that sat low in the water with a forty-horse outboard and a steering wheel.

I reached into my pocket, took out a fifty, and dropped it in his shirt pocket along with my card. "Thanks for your time today, Julio. There's another fifty in it for you if you call us when you see him again."

"*Gracias, señor,*" Julio said before returning to his air-conditioned trailer.

"What shall we do now, partner?" I asked Jim.

"I noticed a restaurant a few hundred yards back the way we came. Let's have lunch and think about it," he replied.

"Perfect," I said as we wandered alongside the dusty road.

THE SPECIAL OF the day was fish tacos, and that's what we ordered, along with two Modelos. After savoring the first sips of the cold, refreshing beer, we glanced at our surroundings. We had a nice ocean view, but we were practically on the road. Every car or truck that went by kicked up dust, and I could feel the grit land on my face.

After moving further from the road, Jim said, "If he shows up this afternoon, at least we'll be close by."

"It sounds like we're making enough progress to spend another day or two."

"For sure. He was just here yesterday, and it sounds like he plans to hang around. We should know soon enough."

"Okay, we'll hang out. Just remember, we don't have weapons."

"Yeah, I guess I'm okay with that. This is a long way from town, though. If we need to act fast, our hotel is too far from here."

"We'll figure that out after lunch. Maybe we should move somewhere in between."

"All I saw on the way here were those big resorts," he said.

"Well, the clients are aware this is plus expenses."

Soon, our food was set before us. The taco shells were soft and warm, the ingredients fresh and crisp, and we were told the fish was fresh Dorado, which I knew was the same as Mahi. Each order came with three tacos and fried plantains—delicious. Neither of us could finish it all, and we sat back in our chairs to stretch our bellies. Moments later, my phone lit up.

"*Señor Burnett?*"

"Yes."

"This is Julio at the boat dock. Your man was just here and rented a boat."

"Is he still there?"

"He just left."

"We'll be right there."

I threw some cash on the table, plenty to cover the tab, and we hurried back to Pacifico Boat Rentals. Not quite running, but walking as fast as our full stomachs allowed, our legs still tired from yesterday. Julio was waiting for us as we approached his trailer.

"Did he say where he was going?" I asked, handing him a fifty.

"No, but he asked how much fuel was aboard. It sounded like he'd be out for the rest of the day."

"We'll rent a boat. We want something bigger and faster than the one he has."

He nodded and gestured for us to follow him to the dock so he could show us what was available. There were two more boats like the ones Gary had rented, and a twenty-two-footer with a small cabin forward and a seventy-five-horsepower outboard.

Pointing to the larger boat, I asked, "Is this one faster?"

"*Sí*. And it can go in bigger seas."

"Fill it up. We'll take it."

"*Sí*." He began carrying five-gallon fuel jugs from a pump near the trailer down the dock to the boat. I asked how many more it would take, and he just shrugged. Jim and I lugged two more down the pier as Julio poured them into the tank. The process took longer than we had hoped, but we wanted as much fuel as possible. Julio declared it full with one jug remaining, and I told him to leave it aboard as a spare.

Jim inspected the boat while I followed Julio to the trailer to fill out a rental form and pay with a credit card. Then, I thought to ask if Gary had given him a credit card.

"No, *señor*. He gave me a thousand-dollar cash deposit."

"Did you get any kind of ID from him?"

"*Sí.*" He rummaged through some papers and said, "A driver's license; Gary Leonard, from New York."

So, without using a credit card, MacKenzie wouldn't know of his location, but I'd now confirmed this was our guy. Julio gave me a map of the area and pointed out a shallow area to watch out for. Then, he followed me back to the boat with a cooler filled with ice and a twelve-pack of bottled water.

"Do you want *cervezas*?"

"No thanks, Julio. Which way did he go?"

"*Norte*," he said, pointing.

Without another word, I started the engine while Julio untied us. A minute later, we were outside the breakwater and heading to sea.

Jim announced, "I found life jackets and a flare gun under the seat. There's also a handheld VHF radio, an anchor, and a paddle by your feet."

"Good to know. Let's open her up and see what she'll do," I said, jamming the throttle forward.

The bow rose as we surged ahead, then settled back down as our speed increased. Within a few seconds, we were skipping along the top of the waves, leaving hardly any wake. I was pleased with the boat's performance.

"How much of a head start do you think he got?" I asked, raising my voice to be heard over the roaring outboard.

"Probably an hour by the time we filled her up."

Sitting behind the windshield, I looked at the map, trying to determine our location. The shallow area Julio warned me about was a reef marked by a buoy on the map. Looking forward, I saw the buoy and steered slightly to port to go around it. Once clear, we resumed our course northward, about a quarter mile offshore. Knowing our location on the map, we looked for small coves where Gary may have gone.

"How long will our fuel last?" Jim inquired.

"We watched him pour fifteen gallons in, and we have another five as a spare. I have no idea what was in the tank to start with. Even though the gauge shows full, I wouldn't trust it. Maybe I should back off the throttle a bit to conserve fuel."

I brought it back to a comfortable cruise speed, still on plane and riding the wave tops. I thought we'd be faster than Gary in his smaller boat while extending our range. Jim searched the chart for any place ahead where Gary might be going. Nothing jumped out at us on the chart, and we didn't see much traffic on the water. Sometimes, you might see a cluster of boats working a popular fishing spot, but not today. We continued, following the shoreline, hoping to catch up to him.

Jim was the first to spot an object ahead as we scanned the horizon. I estimated the range to be about five miles. Maintaining our speed, I could see we were getting closer, but not yet close enough to identify the boat. Soon, I realized it was heading toward us and closing fast. Shortly after that, I knew it wasn't Gary's boat, as we saw a cigarette-style speed boat in excess of forty feet long with two couples aboard, their hair streaming backward at over fifty miles per hour. They waved as they passed, leaving us with the deafening thunder of V-8 engine exhaust.

Disappointed it wasn't Gary, my anticipation continued to build. I knew we were close, yet so far, he'd remained outside our grasp. We continued north for another hour until we noticed a small boat pulled up on the beach in a cove, which again piqued our excitement. As we slowed and went close enough to see if it looked like one of Julio's boats, we saw a man and woman sunbathing nude on the secluded beach. When they noticed us, the woman scrambled to put on her bikini, and we waved before heading out, regretful to have disturbed them.

Checking the time, we realized that if we planned to return to Julio's dock before dark, we would need to turn around soon. We also began to doubt that Gary was even ahead of us. Maybe he had not continued north, or we had missed him somehow, and he'd returned to the dock. Before committing to an overnight stay on a small boat in the Pacific Ocean, we would need to know for sure.

I checked my phone, saw I had three bars of reception, and called Julio. "By any chance, has Gary returned?"

"No, *señor.*"

"What happens if we don't get back before dark?"

"All boats must be in before dark. It's in our agreement."

"I know, but we might not make it."

"You're on your own then. I leave at dark."

"I understand. We'll just tie her up and check with you tomorrow. Will you call me if the other boat returns?"

"*Sí.*"

Looking at the chart again, Jim saw a small town about ten miles ahead that appeared to have a marina. It looked like a likely place Gary would have gone, so we decided to continue. If he wasn't there, we could at least refuel.

A half-hour later, we entered the cove and spotted the marina, which had a fuel dock and a bar and grill a few steps up on the shore. We tied up at the dock and told the attendant to fill her up. While he was doing that, I asked if he had seen someone in a sixteen-foot runabout.

"*Sí*. Maybe a half hour ago."

"Did he say where he was heading?"

"He asked how far it was to Cabo."

"What did you tell him?"

"I said it was nearly two hundred miles, and he'd never make it in that little boat. There's a storm coming tonight, and the seas will be too big."

It took twenty-five gallons to fill the tank. I looked under the back seat to see how big the tank was and saw a label stating it held fifty gallons. I also saw another five-gallon spare tank that felt full when I lifted it. After doing some quick calculations of our fuel burn, I estimated that we had about five hours of fuel on board, plus the spare and our extra jug—possibly an additional hour if we kept our speed down.

"Do you have any fuel jugs we can buy?" I asked.

"No. *Perdón, señor.*"

While I paid for the fuel, Jim went to the bar for sandwiches. A few minutes later, he came out with a bag of cheeseburgers and French fries. We headed back out and continued north at the same cruising speed we had maintained all day. Based on the time interval when Gary refueled, we'd gained a half hour on him in two and a half hours. Not much, but at least we knew we were on the right track. We then scarfed down the burgers and fries while they were still warm.

I turned the wheel over to Jim and dug out the chart. The back side was smaller in scale and showed the Yucatan Peninsula with Cabo San Lucas at the southern tip. The trip would be almost one hundred thirty miles if we went directly there. Another option would be to stay along the coast until reaching the closest distance across the open water, adding about twenty miles to the trip. Regardless of the route, we didn't have enough fuel to make it. We decided to hug the coast and refuel again, hoping Gary did the same.

Thinking about my previous experience with trips of this distance, I was always in a sailboat. Of course, it took a lot longer, but you weren't reliant on fuel, and the boats were designed to handle open seas. This boat was better suited to a lake. With the chart in my lap, I searched for another place to refuel and saw one about twenty miles ahead, near the closest point to Cabo. It was now 5:30, and heavy charcoal-gray clouds were rolling in. I thought we could make it before dark.

We saw some sails on the horizon over the next hour, and as the sun began to set, we approached the bay where our fuel stop was located. On our way in, a small boat was coming out. Again my excitement piqued, and as we passed, I exclaimed, "Shit, that's Gary!"

Jim swung the boat around and followed. Gary appeared to be heading due west, toward Cabo. "Let's overtake him and cut him off!" I exclaimed.

As we raced toward Gary, Jim said, "We're running out of daylight—let's get this done before dark."

As we sped up and our intentions became clear, Gary raised a pistol and began shooting at us. Jim immediately pulled back the throttle, and our boat settled in the water. We had made the mistake of assuming that because we didn't have guns, neither did he.

I briefly considered returning fire with our flare gun, but I knew the accuracy would be poor, and his distance was increasing by the second. "Shit! We don't have the fuel to make it to Cabo!" I exclaimed. "So close yet so far!"

Jim said, "We have no choice but to head for the marina."

Within a few minutes, we were tied to the fuel dock. Our initial thought was just to refuel and go, but by the time we had filled up, it was completely dark and had begun to rain. In barely understandable English, the dock attendant told us the rain would continue most of the night, and the wind would increase to thirty knots. I knew that meant ten-foot seas and building the longer the wind lasted—no place for a lake boat. When I explained the imminent conditions to Jim, he tipped his head and cracked his neck.

We decided to stay right where we were and asked the dock attendant if there was a place to escape the rain. He told us we were welcome to sit in the dock shack, which was just a thatched roof he used for protection from the sun. As it began to rain harder, we took him up on his offer, and he said, "*Buena suerte*," before heading home for the night.

I asked Jim, "Did that mean good night?"

"I think it meant good luck!"

Thankful that we'd eaten when we did, we settled in with bottles of water from our cooler. Unable to sleep sitting in folding chairs, we tried to lie on the wooden deck with a few cushions from our boat, but the rain splashing off the deck became too much. Glancing around, I spotted a sport-fishing boat with settees under a roof. We took shelter there from the howling wind and rain for the rest of the night. It was a cold, miserable experience, and soaked to our underwear, I became depressed, tempted to fly home first thing in the morning.

In the early hours, the rain stopped, and the wind began to taper off. We slept until sunrise, then walked up to use the marina's facilities. Spotting a washer and dryer, we removed our wet clothing, ran it through the dryer, and then dried ourselves off the best we could using paper towels. The warm, dry clothing felt luxurious when we put it back on, and we returned to our boat, feeling comfortable again as we headed for Cabo.

CHAPTER 24

The seas had grown substantially since the day before. I could not imagine what it was like for Gary in that little boat without a windshield in heavy rain and thirty-knot winds. The rain must have felt like nails hitting his face. I imagined that while steering in the dark with waves this size, he would repeatedly become disoriented and unable to maintain a heading. That's if he was lucky enough not to be tossed overboard. It was then that I realized I'd be just as happy finding Gary floating on the surface as I'd be capturing him alive.

Our twenty-two-foot boat climbed up the face of each wave, teetered at the top, and then surfed down the back side. It'd be slow going today, and I was concerned that we'd use more fuel due to the effort of cresting the waves. At least it was daylight, and we could see where we were going.

Soon, we both felt seasick, and Jim began puking over the side. With nothing but water in his stomach, it quickly became dry heaves. I told him about keeping his eyes on the horizon, and within minutes, he felt better. But still, his face was gray as we struggled up the waves, one at a time.

This simple boat had neither a GPS nor a sophisticated chart plotter. We'd be crossing the Gulf of California with just a compass.

After figuring out the direct course, we headed five degrees north to ensure we didn't miss the peninsula altogether. We listened to the weather forecast on the VHF radio and were encouraged to hear of fair weather to come. With the wind settling down, I knew the waves would also, but didn't know how long that would take. We continued west, climbing the waves with the sun on our backs. The flock of seagulls following us had long since given up.

I switched the radio to channel 16 to monitor emergency traffic, thinking Gary might be desperate or dumb enough to call for help. But we heard no distress calls over the next hour. Now that Jim was feeling better, we were starving and mad at ourselves for not staying at the marina long enough for the restaurant to open. Had we waited, the seas would have diminished as well. By 10:00, I estimated we were a third of the way to Cabo, and the seas were still more significant than I had hoped.

An hour later, Jim spotted a reflection ahead but then lost it. We both focused on that spot until it appeared again and turned a few degrees to the south, heading directly for it. As we got closer, we were sure there was something in the water, and once within a thousand yards, we saw someone sitting on top of an overturned boat, waving his arms. It was Gary.

When he figured out who we were, he began shooting at us again. Jim and I knew how far to stay away from pistol fire, and after a few more misses, the gunfire stopped. He had either given up or run out of bullets. We just sat and waited for him to come to his senses. As far as he knew, we were his only hope of being rescued.

"I think we've got him now," Jim said.

"Yeah, he's out of options. He can either be rescued by us, or bake in the sun and die of dehydration."

A half-hour later, we moved closer in hopes of communicating. Jim hollered, "Throw your gun in the water!"

"I already did!" Gary yelled back.

We'd been watching closely and didn't believe him, unless the gun had just slipped down the overturned hull. We then noticed gasoline floating on the surface and maneuvered back to a safe distance, prepared to wait him out. If he jumped in the water and began swimming toward us, we thought it would be safe to pick him up.

That never happened. By mid-afternoon, considering our distance from shore, the approaching darkness, and fearing another uncomfortable night, we needed to bring this situation to a head.

"Fuck this!" Jim said as he reached under the seat and took out the flare gun. He loaded a cartridge and fired at Gary's boat. Instantly, the floating gasoline ignited, and a woof of flame surrounded him. We were close enough to see the panic on his face and watched as Gary searched for a spot in the water that was not on fire. When he found one, he dove in and began swimming toward us. Once he got closer, we maneuvered alongside, allowing him to cling to the side of the boat. With our engine running, we could ditch him at any moment if he became hostile.

If we had handcuffs with us, we would have put them on his wrists and pulled him aboard. Without them, I improvised with a dock line. With his hands clinging to the rail, I wrapped it around both wrists and pulled it through a loop that tightened the more I pulled. It was a knot I had learned to attach a small line to a larger one. Once he was restrained, we pulled him aboard, laid him on the back seat, and tied his ankles to a cleat on the other side with another dock line. Once secured, we turned and headed back to the mainland.

A few minutes later, Jim moved close to my ear and said softly, "Once we turn him over to the Feebs, we may never know how this all went down. Now's our chance to find out while we have some leverage."

"You're absolutely right, partner," I said before pulling back the throttle and coming to a stop. After shutting down the engine, I turned my seat around to face Gary and announced, "You're going to tell us how each and every one of those young women died."

After a moment, he said, "I had nothing to do with it."

As our boat wallowed in the water, he looked away from me, unwilling to make eye contact like the pitiful excuse for a human being he was. I grabbed the paddle, stood up, and whacked him in the face with the flat side. We heard a crunch, maybe from his nose breaking. When he brought his bound hands up to his face for protection, I struck him in the gut, this time with the edge of the paddle, knocking the breath out of him. As he gasped for air, he rolled on his side to protect his belly, and I struck him in the kidneys, again with the edge. *Hard*. He cried out in pain as I stood over him, ready to strike again.

"Okay, okay." Struggling to breathe, we heard, "What do you want to know?"

"We want to know everything," I replied.

"Aren't you going to read me my rights?" he gasped.

Jim and I burst out laughing. I tried to reply but was too consumed by the hilarity of the moment, bent over, clutching my belly. Gary just looked at us with the eyes of a weasel.

Eventually, Jim was able to speak. "We're not the cops, asshole, and we're in fucking Mexico. Even if we were cops, we could just dump you overboard. With your hands and feet tied, you'd drown in thirty seconds—and no one would ever know!" Jim again roared with laughter.

When I'd gathered myself, I said, "We're your only hope for survival, moron. If you don't tell us what we want to know, we'll toss you in, just like you tossed in those young ladies." When he finally made eye contact, I said, "First, tell us about Amy."

It took a while, but after coming to grips with his defeat, Gary said, "It all started with Amy. On the Fourth of July, I took her out on my boat to watch the fireworks and drink some beers. After they ended, we went back to my house, and I fucked her. It was then, that very first time, she asked me to choke her. At first, I just put my hand around her neck, but she demanded I really choke her so she couldn't breathe. I've never seen someone come like that before—she was out of control, screaming and thrashing, with her face beet red."

Gary then stopped speaking, maybe hoping he was done.

"Keep going."

"Over the next few weeks, she couldn't get enough, and she taught me all about it and did it to me. I sorta got into it. Then, one day, Amy brought over a choking collar and chain and wanted me to bolt it to the ceiling over the bed so we could hang each other during sex. She loved it! One thing led to another, and we created a bondage room at my lake house, and she brought over all those devices, including the Sybian."

"What happened next?"

"She started bringing her friends over to try out the Sybian. The first was Laura Kelly, a nurse she went to school with. I think it was the second time she was there that the three of us had sex together. Amy choked her so hard her eyes rolled back, and she stopped breathing. Amy tried to revive her with CPR, but we couldn't save her. We brought Laura back to my house, rolled her up in a rug, loaded her in the boat, and dumped her in the Sound.

"Who was next?"

He feigned having difficulty remembering but eventually said, "Natalie Morgan. She was really into the threesome thing, and after a few occasions, Amy choked her to death when she came. We again dumped the body in the Sound."

"That's two. Continue."

"After Natalie, Amy found Sierra on a BDSM website. I never met her, but Amy brought her to the lake house to ride the Sybian with the choke collar. Amy told me Sierra was so into the asphyxiation that she hung herself. Amy thought it was the hottest thing she'd ever seen—she called it 'death by orgasm.'"

"Okay, you're doing well. Who was next?"

"A few days later, Amy planned to meet me at the lake house to dispose of Sierra's body. But when I arrived, I found Amy hanging from the choke collar over the Sybian with a broken neck. I loaded them both in my boat and dumped them in the Sound."

Jim and I looked at each other, suspicious. The way Gary told it, he wasn't responsible for any of the deaths. It was all Amy's doing, and he just helped dispose of the bodies.

"Tell us about Melinda Bernardi," I said, watching closely for his reaction.

"I never met her either. Amy said she choked her to death with her hands and asked me to get rid of the body."

"Whoa, asshole. Your story places all the blame on Amy, but we know she was already gone before Melinda disappeared."

"That can't be right."

I struck him again in the face with the paddle, this time splitting his right eyebrow. As blood ran down his face, I said, "Let's toss him in, Jim."

Jim prepared to untie Gary's legs from the cleat when Gary blurted," All right! I killed her."

"Talk to us."

He groaned, "Amy had shown me her posts on the website and how to access them. Melinda replied to a post, and I met her and brought her to the lake house."

"Then what happened?"

"We fucked for two days while I kept her tied up. On the third day, I choked her until she passed out, and she never came around."

"Okay, so you admit to killing her?"

Gary hesitated to answer, and I raised the paddle, ready to strike again. "Yes! Yes, I killed her!"

"How about Ariana Alonzo?"

"Amy's website post had expired by then, so I posted one of my own. Ariana responded a week later and said she was into breath play. She told me we could go to a vacant house and have sex. The next morning, we met at her office, and she took me to a big fancy house for sale. She wanted me to hold my hand over her mouth and pinch her nose closed when she came. She loved it. A few minutes later, when I was about to bust a nut, I got carried away and choked her too hard."

"So that's two women that you admit to killing," I stated.

He said nothing.

"How about Jenifer, the girl we found tied up at your lake house?"

"She also responded to my post."

"And you would have ended up killing her, too?"

"I never intended to harm anyone. They all enjoyed it; I just got carried away sometimes."

"Is that the way it was with your wife, Maria?"

"I loved Maria. She was just so fragile."

Having heard his account of all the deaths, Jim and I looked at each other, and then I started the engine and headed for the mainland. Other than his attempted lie about Melinda, his story aligned with the facts as I knew them. I didn't know how much of it was true, but that would be up to real cops and the courts to determine. I was content with the confession we got.

ABOUT AN HOUR out, when I had cell service, I called Agent MacKenzie. When he answered, I asked, "Would you like to take custody of Gary Leonard in Mexico?"

"Son of a bitch. Where are you?"

"A couple of hours north of Puerto Vallarta. I'll call with the exact location when we reach a marina."

"You're on a boat?" he asked.

"That's correct. He was trying to cross the Gulf of California when his boat capsized in a storm."

"And you just happened to be standing by to rescue him?"

"Something like that. I'll call you in an hour," I said before hanging up.

CHAPTER 25

Mia and I were lying in bed, in post-coital bliss, at a hotel in Rome across from the Pantheon. She had just worked for two days in Milan, and now she got to spend the Christmas holiday with me—a national hero.

As fate would have it, Jim and I traveled back to JFK on the same flight as Special Agent MacKenzie and his fugitive, Gary Leonard. It was by pure happenstance. Upon arrival, the media swarmed Agent MacKenzie as he led his handcuffed prisoner, with black eyes and a bandaged eyebrow, through the gate.

While praising MacKenzie for tracking down "The Nurse Murderer," they asked how he found him, and he pointed at me across the room as Jim and I tried to avoid the cameras. As the swarm headed for us, Jim managed to slip away when the media had me cornered. I answered their questions, praising the FBI and the cooperation from the Mexican Police. I managed to mention the fine work of Detectives Willy Grant and Bella Fratelli from the 50th Precinct in the Bronx, along with my partner Jim Abbott. I even got some kudos in for Frosty.

The media played that loop repeatedly on the national news for the next few days, placing the spotlight on me for just doing what I was hired to do. Uncomfortable in my five minutes of fame, this time, when Mia asked me to go to Italy with her, I jumped at the chance.

WE SPENT THE week after Christmas wandering the streets of Rome from one historic site to another, in mild temperatures just right for a light jacket. She had been there before and proved to be an excellent tour guide. Known as the Eternal City and the home of Catholicism, Christmas in Rome was a time for celebration. Nativity scenes were set up throughout the city, and beautifully decorated Christmas trees adorned every corner. She took me to the Colosseum, which I found fascinating, and we spent an entire afternoon wandering around the Roman Forum, an ancient collection of architectural relics.

We toured St. Peter's Cathedral, where its sheer size amazed me, as did the sculptures by Bernini and Michelangelo. We climbed the stairs in St. Peter's all the way to the top. Along the way, we could reach out and touch the frescos that appeared to be paintings from the main floor but were ceramic tile chips embedded in the plaster. Mia knew better than to attempt to see the Sistine Chapel during such a busy week—the line was around the block. She took me to a few of her favorite restaurants, tucked away from the crowds, and we discovered a few of our own.

Our favorite place of all was Piazza Navona. This vast public square featured baroque architecture, historic fountains, and great people-watching. We sat at tables along the sidewalk almost every day, sipping Aperol Spritzes while enjoying the Christmas celebrations. If I were to live in Rome, I would want to be within walking distance of this delightful place.

During our week there, we must have walked a dozen miles, stopping for espresso here and gelato there. Some of what we saw was two thousand years old—just incredible.

By the time we returned to New York, Mia was already planning our next trip to Europe.

Thank you for reading *Breath Play*

If you enjoyed the book, please leave an Amazon Review!

You may follow the author at
www.larryterhaar.com

Other titles by this Author:

Against the Blue Wall https://a.co/d/2duKj5p
Once a Detective... https://a.co/d/jf0pO3n
Oceanside https://a.co/d/eAMb3cG

ACKNOWLEGEMENTS

My sincere thanks to all those who helped me bring this book
to publication.

Proofreading by Larry Butler

Formatting by Trisha Fuentes

Book Cover by Zizi Subiyarta

My advanced reading team for posting early reviews

(You know who you are.)

A special thanks to my editor, Emma Collins

And as always, I dedicate this book to my wife, Beth, whose support
makes everything possible.